Silver-Gem

"Gem-esis"

By: Russ Shumshinov

Published by:

Team Silver-Gem LLC

ISBN #: 978-1-7334160-0-9

Copyright © 2019 Ruslan Shumshinov

All Rights Reserved

Cover Design: Concept: Author / Final: Tim Findling

Help With Finalizing and Formating for Publishing: Todd Brockdorf

Everything else, by yours truly.

Disclaimer:

Everything you are about to read is imaginary. A work of fiction. All names, characters, places, events, companies, institutions and conversations; are mere figments of the author's very creative and sometimes disturbing imagination. The views and ideas expressed within, are those of fictional characters and their imaginations. Any and all references to existing products or characters, are for informational, narrative, and/or transformative purposes only. It is not the author's intent to belittle, degrade, insult or defame, any of the fore mentioned. Not intended as: parental advice, medical advice, investment advice, or any other form of advice, whatsoever.

Quite honestly, I find it a bit concerning that I even have to say this but, here it goes:

!!!WARNING!!!

Do not try anything you are about to read at home or anywhere else, for that matter!!!

The characters are fictitious! The things they do will kill you!

There, now that we've got that all out of the way; I hope you enjoy reading the story, as much as I did writing it.

To my family, without whose inspiration, the story wouldn't exist.

And,

In loving memory of my friend,

Jeffrey David Wadha.

Who's probably looking down from heaven with a smile; yelling, "It's about fuckin' time!"

CHAPTER ONE:

INTRODUCTIONS

[Man standing in front of a mirror and tying his tie. He is looking at the reflection of his wife, who is still sleeping in the bed.]

Look at her, that resting lioness. Kind, caring, beautiful, sexy, brilliant…[she snores]. But she can also be fierce, trust me, I've pissed her off enough times to know. She may not look it but, she is one of the strongest people I've ever met. I knew that she was the one the moment I saw her. Unfortunately, she didn't see it, at first. I must have asked her out twenty times in twenty ways before she finally agreed to go out with me. How did I finally convince her? I told her that I thought we were perfect for each other and that we will never know for sure, unless she gives me a chance. I told her, "Just give me one hour to show you why we're perfect for each other. And after that, if you don't agree, I will never bother you again.". I'm not really sure which part of that changed her mind but, I'm glad it worked. Then, I did what any smart man would do; I married her and locked-that-shit-in, before she came to her senses.

We've been married for over ten years. Been through our ups and downs and always found a way to handle life's little shit-bombs gracefully. She works as a dental hygienist and makes a pretty decent living. But, she really stepped-up during those years when I was trying to build a clientele for my business. She always steps-up when needed. She's been nothing but a great wife, best friend, a wonderful partner and a perfect mother. She also gave me the two greatest gifts I could've ever wanted, my two boys, Samuel and Jeffrey.

Sammy was the first to pop out. I named him Samuel after Mark Twain (look it up) because, the man was a witty genius, who never gave-up and always did things his way. He's only eight-years old and is already exactly like me. I mean, if they were to clone me, he's what would come out. Really, in his 3-month ultrasound, he already had my profile. My swimmers are awesome. He acts like me, thinks like me, speaks like me and, much to my dismay, even argues like me. He is very smart but, sometimes over thinks things (just like I do), funny, creative and curious.

Our second bundle of joy, Jeffrey, arrived twenty months later. I named him Jeffrey after my friend Jeffrey David Wadha. Jeff was the best friend I ever had until, at the age of thirty-eight, just three months before my son Jeffrey was born, cancer took him from us. FUCKING CANCER!!! I miss my friend and I wanted a constant reminder of him. The funny thing is, Jeffrey's behaviors, positive attitude and outlook on life are just like my friend's were. He's clever, very social, vocal, funny and talks with his hands. It sometimes makes me think that Jeff's been reincarnated into Jeffrey. That would be awesome.

These boys are amazing. We taught them to speak Russian first, and they love it. Because, they can tell each-other "secrets" without other kids understanding them. But, since preschool, they've been learning English. And at this age, they pick-up everything; words, tones, gestures; especially the ones you hoped they would miss. To this day, they think that "God damn it!" means to be quiet or to calm down, "asshole" means inconsiderate, "shit" is something you say when you're angry, disappointed or scared, "suck-it" is just a rude way to tell someone "no thank you", and "the finger" is a way to tell someone to watch what they're saying or doing. I know it's bad but, at this point, what else am I to do? Tell them that those are bad things to say or gesture? No fucking way! I'm not going to be that dick-head who thinks that explaining the "true" meaning of these things to his kids is a good idea. I have two boys; they thrive on this kind of thing. All telling them the "truth" will do, is make them say and do the things even more, and even worse, out of context. I'm just happy they haven't got the "F" word yet, you know the one, "FUCK". One of my all-time favorites. Truly, one of the most versatile words in the English language. It can be used by itself or combined with a multitude of creative hyphenations, to say just about anything. It's been the hardest word for me to (try to) stop saying around my kids. I literally had to increase my vocabulary by a hundred words or more, just to make-up for that one. Now, they have heard it before, either from me or some of the music we listen to but, I always find a way to cover it up. Wonder how long that's going to last. I mean, I'm with them all the time. I love hanging-out with them, even when I'm not actively participating in their activities. Now, some guys don't like to hang-out with their kids because it's "boring". I beg to fuckin' differ. If you think that kids are "boring", then you're not paying attention. I love watching them, hearing them, playing with them. Every day is like a new adventure. Plus, they keep you from looking like an idiot, when you act like a kid.

I teach my kids to be polite, courteous and to always try to do the right thing. And like most parents, I don't always practice what I preach. To me, pretty much everyone outside of my inner circle is an asshole, until proven otherwise. You see, I've always had an over-developed sense of justice. Which means, that I always try to do the right thing, I just haven't always been too nice about it. But what I've come to realize, is that when you're also nice to people, and I mean genuinely (not that fake smile and "how are you" bullshit), it in turn has the effect of making you have to go to extremes less often. In addition, doing the right thing makes you feel confident, proud and empowered as a person. The trick is, not to become someone's bitch in the process. Otherwise, it gets harder and harder to do the right thing. And then, you snap. And when I snap, it's not good for anybody.

    Most importantly, you have to understand that once you have kids, you're no longer the most important thing in your life. If you can't handle that, don't have kids. As far as I'm concerned, these amazing boys and this wonderful woman, are the best things in my life. I love them, I live for them and I would die for them.

    [Sammy comes into the room.]

    Sammy - "Papa, you owe me five-dollars."

    Gem - "Five-whole-dollars? For what?"

    [Sammy smiles. Another front tooth fell out.]

    That's right. My kids know there's no such thing as the "Tooth-Fairy". My wife gets pissed at me because, I don't let my boys believe in fairy tales. She, like most other parents, thinks that it's better for them to "enjoy the fantasy" for a while. Fuck that! Why tell them lies now just to break their little hearts later? Besides, I'm sure there's plenty of real shit out there, that's even more fantastic than the fairy tales. That's what I want them to focus on. So, how did I handle it? When he lost his first tooth, he told me that the other kids in school told him, that he has to put it under his pillow to get money from the "Tooth Fairy". And this is what transpired:

[Flashback:]

Gem - "Tooth-Fairy? There's no such thing as a 'Tooth-Fairy'. That was just their parents, taking their teeth and giving them money."

[Sammy looked disappointed. Jeffrey, who was standing right next to him, looked sad. Gem's wife, gives him a mean look because he "ruined it" for the boys.]

Gem - "So, how much did this supposed 'Tooth-Fairy' give your friends?"

Sammy - "I don't know…some kids said fifty-cents, some kids got a dollar, some got two."

Gem - "That's it?! I would think a tooth's worth more than that! I'll tell you what, you get that tooth to me and I'll give you five-dollars. Okay?"

[Sammy looks at Jeffrey in excitement. Jeffrey smiles back. Sammy looks back at his father.]

Sammy - "Yeah! Screw the Tooth-Fairy! I want your deal."

[Back to present time.]

And that's how I handled that situation. I love a win/win.

[Sammy hands Gem his tooth. Gem hands him a twenty. Sammy takes the money, smiles and runs away.]

Gem - "I want my change."

Sammy - "No. Just don't pay me for the next three."

He said that because he knows I'll forget.

[Jeffrey enters Gem's room.]

Jeffrey - "Why was Sammy happy so early in the morning?"

Gem - "Because, he just got paid for another tooth."

[Jeffrey walks over and looks at a vase full of wilting flowers.]

Jeffrey - "Hey! What the heck?! These flowers are dying."

Ahhh…those fucking flowers. Like most women, my wife loves getting flowers but, I hate buying them. What's the point? I'd rather spend the money on something that lasts, like jewelry or…okay, pretty much just jewelry. So, a little over a week ago, my boys decided they wanted to buy their mom flowers for her birthday. They got their money together and bought her a beautiful bouquet. And now, the harsh reality hits.

Jeffrey - "Papa look, the flowers are dying. They're dry and there's no water in the vase. I don't think that mom even took care of them. She probably didn't feed them or water them."

[Jeffrey lifts his hands in disbelief.]

Jeffrey - "What kind of person does that?!"

Gem - "Jeffrey, mom did everything she could to keep them alive and fresh, as long as possible."

Jeffrey - "So, why are they dying?"

Gem - "They always do. They last a week or two, then they dye. That's just what happens."

Jeffrey - "Always?"

Gem - "Always."

Jeffrey - "Then, why did we buy them? What a waste of money. I'm never doing that again."

Gem - "Thank you. Now you get it. Now, go get dressed. Mom's taking you guys to school today."

[Jeffrey runs off to get dressed. Natasha is sitting up in bed, shaking her head at Gem.]

Natasha - "Why do you teach them these things?"

Gem - "I don't. Life does. I just point it out so they don't miss it."

[Gem kisses Natasha and goes down to the kitchen. He makes his morning coffee, kisses the boys good-bye and heads out to the garage.]

And, who the fuck am I? I'm a forty-five-year-old, Russian immigrant, husband to one, father of two. My real name is Raphael Simonov but, everyone calls me "Gem". Why Gem? Well, my asshole friend Victor started calling me that about fifteen years ago and it just stuck. He said he called me that because I'm an unstable Gemini. This from an ex-KGB operative who makes his money through his "social clubs". Which are basically really nice versions of a casino/brothel/bar/night club all in one. I like to tell people that I got my nickname by being brilliant, valuable and hard as a gem stone. Not everyone believes that story. But enough about that dick, for now. I'm sure we'll get to him later. I'm running late for work.

[Gem gets into his car and starts driving.]

I love my job. As long as I have a secure and stable Internet connection and a smart-phone, ninety percent of what I do can be done from anywhere. This gives me the freedom to spend time with my family and still earn a good living. I can drop the boys off at school, pick them up, take them to all their "extra-curriculars" and be home with them for every meal. I love it! But, it hasn't always been this way.

I used to work crazy hours and hardly ever got to spend any quality time with them. I'm talking extended shifts every day, 5:00 A.M. to 6:00 P.M., six days a week. I was always so tired, that I would fall asleep in the middle of everything; bed time stories, dinner and even playtime. What kind of shit is that? It was killing me. So, I took a risk and started managing money for other people. I've done it for years for myself and family, with pretty impressive results (if I do say so myself). I got licensed, got a job at a "boutique" money management firm and got some money together. Then, after several years of grinding it out, I created a proprietary style which protects assets while they grow and provides the investor with monthly income that out-performs most other fixed income investments. And all that while staying "liquid". A few years later, my styles performance was stellar. It is the slow, steady and safe approach to investments that big money loves. And love it they did. So much so, that I was no longer going fishing for business, the fish were jumping in the boat themselves.

That's actually why I'm going into the office today. My first "whale" account, Lockhart Industries, just recently lost its founder,

Chairman and C.E.O., Mr. John Lockhart. I was heartbroken when he passed. He was a class act; a good man with a big heart. His advice on life, family, money; made me a better man. And all the business he sent my way, over the years, made me a richer man. His death shocked everyone. His health was great, his mind was sharp and he had more energy than a six-year-old on a sugar high. No-one saw it coming. Their board is supposed to meet this morning to elect a new chairman and CEO. My money is on Mr. Lockhart's son, John Lockhart, Jr.. That guy's a shoe-in! He loves their company, he knows it inside-out, he's got a great business acumen, a great personality and the employees love him. He'll have big shoes to fill but, I think he's a perfect fit for the job. It would take an act of God, for him not to take over the helm.

[Gem gets to the office / walking towards his work area.]

Well, here we are. This is my office. That is my workstation; fuckin' thing hasn't been turned on in months. And, that is my assistant, Tommy. His real name is Tamis-raha-something or other; (it means "Destroying Darkness" in Hindi / seriously, I couldn't make this shit-up). I love that little guy, even though half the time I don't understand what the fuck he's saying. Partly because of his accent but, mostly because of the shear speed with which the words come out of his mouth. It's like a fuckin' machine gun, "pra-ta-ta-ta-tat". But who gives a shit? He's loyal, hard-working and brilliant. He takes care of all the back-office bullshit that goes on around here and he is currently working on an algorithm for me, that will make my money management style a lot more autonomous. I'll still have to do some occasional tweaking due to political events, natural or man-made disasters and other crap of that nature. Because, you can't program intuition; the gut feeling that will tell you things long before your mind can even wrap itself around the situation.

Tommy - "Gem, your meeting is about to start."

Gem - "On my way."

Tommy - "Would you like me to come, just in case you need my help."

Gem - "Thank you for offering. But, I'm usually pretty good at fucking these things up, all on my own."

[As Gem arrives at the conference room, he sees his boss, Richard Daniels, the Board of Directors for Lockhart Industries and John Jr. standing around the conference room table.]

There's John Junior. Wow! He looks like shit. He's probably still mourning his father. I gotta get over there and check on him.

[As Gem makes his way to John Junior, he hears his boss, Richard Daniels say:]

Richard - "Gentlemen. Please take your seats."

Gem Thinks - "Shit. I guess it'll have to wait."

[John Jr. gets up to speak.]

John Jr. - "I would like to introduce you all to the new Chairman and CEO of Lockhart Industries…"

Gem Thinks - "Is this guy about to intro himself?"

John Jr. - "Mr. Wilhelm Dietrich!"

Gem - "What the fuck?!"

[Everyone looks at Gem.]

Gem - "Sorry. I meant to think that. Just a little surprised, that's all."

Gem Thinks - "Stupid filter."

[Wilhelm stands up and starts to introduce himself. Gem's not paying any attention to him. He's still in shock.]

Gem Thinks - "Ooooooh…look at this fucking guy. What a douche-bag! I mean, if you looked-up the definition of the word in the dictionary:(not the first one, the second one)"

Douche-bag - (noun)

1. A small syringe for douching the vagina, especially as a contraceptive measure

2. [INFORMAL - NORTH AMERICAN]

An obnoxious or contemptible person (typically used for a man)

Gem Thinks - "The only thing missing, is this pompous prick's picture. And he's not just a douche, he's the worst fucking kind: a rich, arrogant, holier-than-thou, master-of-the-universe wanna-be kind of douche. Really, who's dick did this guy have to suck to get this gig?"

[Gem looks around the room and sees a very old and very weird looking man.]

Gem Thinks - "Eww! Not his I hope"

[Wilhelm still talking. Gem still not paying attention. Looking around, still trying to figure out what happened. Spots one of the other board members who looks like he's about to fall asleep.]

Gem Still Fucking Thinking - "I mean, seriously, that dildo over there, looks like he would have been a better choice than this guy."

Wilhelm - "…which brings me to why we're all here today. We are scheduling meetings with many of our current vendors to discuss more favorable terms for our business. Upon recent review, I have noticed that many of the contracts we currently have in place, were negotiated years ago, when the company lacked the magnitude for the favorable treatment that I believe we are entitled to, at this stage of the game. And, in your case, Mr.; I'm sorry, is it Simonov?"

Gem - "Yes. Rafael Simonov. But my friends call me Gem."

Wilhelm - "Gem."

Gem - "Gem."

Wilhelm - "Alright, Mr. Gem…"

Gem - "Simonov is fine."

[Wilhelm looks at Gem with a confused / annoyed face.]

Gem - "I'm just messin' with you. Gem is good."

Wilhelm - "As I was saying, Mr. Gem, I believe it is time for us to renegotiate this outdated contract."

Gem - "I'm sorry, what do you mean 'outdated'?"

Wilhelm - "Like I said, just a minute ago; when this contract was initially drawn-up, we had significantly less under management with you than we do today."

Gem - "Yeah, so?"

Wilhelm - "So therefore, I think that a reduction in your management fees is in order. We have already gone out for bids and most have come in at 15 basis points below your current fee."

Gem - "No."

The way they all looked at me when I said that, you would have thought that I just ripped the loudest fart ever.

Wilhelm - "No?"

Richard - "No?"

Gem - "No!"

Wilhelm - "It is my understanding that our business makes-up a substantial portion of your firm's revenue. And, the way you are reacting to my request, is making me think that you may not appreciate our business as much as you should."

Gem - "And from the way you're acting, I don't think you appreciate me or the work I've done or the money I've made for your company, over these years."

Wilhelm - "You are not the only game in town. I know that Mr. Lockhart and yourself had a very strong relationship. But, unfortunately, Mr. Lockhart is no longer with us. And, unfortunately for you, I do not harbor the same feelings of loyalty toward you as he did. I have absolutely no problem taking our business elsewhere."

[Richard turns to Gem, nervously.]

Richard - "Gem, you really need to reconsider this!"

Gem - "I'm not reconsidering shit! This guy's bluffing!"

[Gem looks at Wilhelm.]

Gem - "Why are you here?"

Wilhelm - "Due to our long-standing relationship with your firm, I wanted to allow you the opportunity to keep our business."

Gem - "Is that right?"

Wilhelm - "Yes."

Gem - "Alright, Willie…"

Wilhelm - "It's Wilhelm."

Gem - "Whatever. You win."

As soon as I said that, that dick smeared an ear-to-ear, gotch-ya smile onto his face. Watch me wipe it right off, that smug mug of his.

Gem - "Take your money and go. Please let me know if you need my help during the transition."

Willie - "I'm sorry but, did I just hear you correctly?"

Richard - "Gem! What the hell are you doing?"

Gem - "I'm not doing anything! Willie's right. We're screwing them big-time. The jig is up. We had a good run. Our days of overcharging for our services, are over."

[Everyone is dumbfounded.]

Gem - "I should be ashamed of myself. I mean, who the hell do I think I am, charging a client of this 'magnitude' 15bps more than anyone else would. I only outperform those other guys by an average of 2% per year. Now, Mr. Willie here, can go back to his shareholders and explain to them why he thinks it's a good idea to lose 2% to save 15bps."

Hey, look, Willie's big smile is gone. Replaced by a "you got me" angry smirk.

Gem - "Isn't that right, Mr. Wilhelm."

[The room is tense. All eyes on Wilhelm.]

Willie - "Okay. You got me but, you can't blame a man for trying."

He was trying to be all nonchalant about it but, you could tell, he was pissed.

Gem - "Whatever, Douche-bag."

[Everyone gets quiet and looks at Gem.]

Shit! I meant to think that. This guy's throwing my mental filter off. Now I gotta pretend I was kidding.

Gem - "Gotch-ya!"

[Everybody has a good, nervous laugh. Willie and Gem are looking at each other. They both know Gem meant it. Meeting ends. People chatting and having refreshments. Gem walks-up to John Jr.]

John Jr. - "Gem, sorry about this meeting. That guy's always trying to prove himself to such an extent that it almost ends up backfiring on him. He thought you'd be an easy target, that's why he wanted you to be his first meeting and why he wanted the entire board to be here. To bear witness to his intellectual prowess. But you handled yourself well. Dad would have been proud."

Gem - "Fuck that guy. I've ruined grander schemes for better people. What I want to know is, what the hell happened last night?"

John Jr. - "I wish I knew. It seems, some of the members had a last-minute change-of-heart. You should have seen them during the vote, it was as if they wanted to but, didn't out of fear, of something."

Gem - "You would have been a perfect choice; and not just a legacy vote but, as somebody who knows the company, inside and out."

John Jr. - "It's OK Gem. I'm over it. Now, it's time to protect the company."

Gem - "How have you been since the funeral?"

John Jr. - "I'm doing okay, all things considered. The family and I are spending a lot of time together. Comforting each other, telling stories…By the way, thank you for everything you and your wife did with the funeral arrangements, it really took a lot of pressure off at the time."

Gem - "You don't have to thank me, John. Your father was a great man, in every way possible. I did for him what I would have done for my own family. I am really gonna miss him."

John Jr. - "You know, dad was always fond of you. He loved your energy and perseverance. He always said, "If Gem could only filter what's in his mind before it comes out of his mouth…""

Gem - "Oh, it's on dude. The filter's on. That little outburst you just witnessed was nothing. I know things get out occasionally but, the difference between what's going on in my mind and what's coming out of my mouth is like the difference between a bazooka and a sling-shoot. Trust me. I could be much worse. You've just never seen me pissed enough."

[Gem looks around the room and sees that everybody is packing up.]

Gem - "What? The party's over? These dinos need a nap already?"

John Jr. - "Yeah, we have to go. He's got four more of these scheduled for today. We'll see how the others go. Maybe, I'll get that CEO spot after all."

Gem - "I've got my fingers crossed for you, buddy. Hey, what do you guys have going on this weekend? I was thinking, maybe get the families together, eat some burgers by the lake, tell war stories about your dad. You know, as hard as it's been on us, it's been hitting the kids even harder. I think it will be good for them."

John Jr. - "I think it would be great for all of us. Unfortunately, the first thing Mr. Wilhelm did as CEO, was assign me to a massive project in Europe. It's a big undertaking. Dad's been working on this project for years and I'm the only one who's been in the loop for every aspect of it. So, from the surface, I understand. But I think that below the surface, there lies another agenda."

Gem - "So, fucked if you do and fucked if you don't."

John Jr. - "I love how you simplify things."

Gem - "John, you go finish your father's work and make him proud. As for this douche-bag; don't worry about him. These overly-ambitious, overly-smart, dick-heads, always find a way to blow themselves-up eventually. And if not, we'll help him along."

John Jr. - "Thanks, Gem. I'll call you as soon as I find out when I'll be home and we'll do that barbecue."

Gem - "Sounds good."

[John Jr. and Gem shake hands and John leaves with the rest of the Lockhart crew. Gem walks out of the conference room, goes back to his "work area" to say "bye" to Tommy and starts walking out of the office.]

That was a great meeting. Seriously, I learned a lot. Like the fact that my favorite account, which used to be headed by one of the nicest and most honorable men you ever met, is now in the hands of an asshole. I wonder what really happened. John Jr. should have been the obvious choice, even for those dildos. But, whatever; for now, it is what it is. I just want to get back home and do some work.

[Gem gets into his car and starts driving home.]

Like I said before, I love what I do. I love trading everything, stocks, bonds, futures; but when it comes to what I love to own, the answer is silver. Yes silver. And no, not the paper shit you get through the futures or even ETF markets. Now I know that they're (supposedly) backed by physical positions but, in the case of a total financial meltdown; how the fuck are you gonna get to it? That's why I'm talking about the physical stuff. The stuff you hold in your hand, the stuff you know you have. Why, you ask? Let me list my reasons:

- Silver is very malleable and can be polished to the highest reflectivity of any metal
- Best conductor of heat and electricity of any other (known) metal
- Has never been worthless

- Other than crude-oil, silver is used in more industrial applications than any other commodity
- Every year, hundreds of millions of ounces of silver become irrecoverable (economically) through industrial applications
- Used in almost every electric appliance
- At current depletion rates, supplies should get pretty scarce in the future
- Great hedge against currency devaluation
- Needed as a catalyst in the plastics making process
- Medicinal use - it's a powerful, non-toxic (when used properly), anti-viral, anti-bacterial and anti-fungal agent / can be mixed with antibiotics or MSM (look it up)
- Big investment banks are loading-up on the physical stuff, as they sell the paper crap to keep the spot value of silver artificially low (follow the big guys / they control this relatively small market)

As you can clearly see, I love the stuff. Although, like everything else, it does have its drawbacks. And as an investment, owning silver can get a bit frustrating:

- Owning silver pays no interest or dividends
- Can get difficult to store and expensive to insure physical stockpiles

- Any substantial price spikes are usually very short lived, followed by years of decline and then, even more years of just sitting around the same levels, doing nothing.

That said, the main reason I buy silver is as an insurance policy. The same reason you buy insurance for your house, car, health, etc.; you dish out money for something you hope you don't have to use anytime soon, (especially true in the case of life insurance). It's protection from the inevitable currency devaluations, caused by the printing of too much money or even worse, defaulting on national debt. And if you think the national debts around the world are out of control, once you tack on another couple hundred-trillion dollars these governments have in unfunded liabilities, you see that it's unsustainable. And unfortunately, this addiction of spending other people's money is a bi-partisan illness. We are spending ourselves silly and the party's not going to end well. So, the dilemma becomes, how do you accumulate the stuff without constantly dishing out new funds? Easy, you have to make the silver pay for itself. And how to do that? Well, you could try to time the markets, tone silver coins and sell them as "art toned" for a few extra bucks or if you have the money to invest in equipment, make and sell your own colloidal silver. I've tried the first two options with some success but, after doing the math, I chose to go with making and selling the colloidal silver.

What is colloidal silver? It is a solution of nano-sized silver particles suspended in water. Why would someone want to buy it? Because of its many medicinal properties. It can be used topically or orally. It is said to destroy all types of bacteria, viruses and fungi, in a way that does not allow them to mutate into "super-bugs". For many years, before the discovery of penicillin, this was the "antibiotic". The process of making colloidal silver, is a simple one. You take some distilled water, drop-in two silver rods, give it the right amount of electricity for a while and, "presto". Because of its ease of manufacture and lots of renewed interest, there are now a ton of companies making the stuff. Why get into a crowded market? Because, after much research, I found a way of making it in a much more consistent manner. Like what Rockefeller did for kerosene, when he made it "standardized", so that each batch is the same as the one before. My method accurately produces the same sized particles and PPM (parts per million) count, for each batch.

[Gem walks into the house and heads for the basement.]

And, what does it take to do all this…?

[Gem turns on the basement lights.]

Ta-da! It's my very own home lab. Complete with all the trimmings. I have an Atomic Absorption Spectrophotometer, to precisely measure any and all metal concentrations in my solutions. A Dynamic Light Scattering apparatus, which measures the size and zeta potential of nano-particles. A pharmaceutical grade, eight stage, water filtration system. An industrial size AC/DC converter with a bridge rectifier, which turns the AC power from my fuse-box into the DC power I need for the process. A super high capacity, ultra-capacitor battery back-up system, which stores the power the system needs to disperse the silver. It takes-up a lot of room but, this thing can store enough power to run a house for a while. And finally, thousands and thousands of ounces of .9999 silver. Why do I prefer the .9999 over the .999? Let me put it this way, what would you rather ingest; a solution with one part of 1,000 being off or a solution with one part in 10,000 being off? That extra "9" does make a difference. All the equipment was installed and tested by ISO certified techs.

There are several ways of making colloidal silver. I can make High Voltage AC (HVAC) colloidal silver, which contains much smaller particles with a higher charge density than conventional DC current produced colloidal silver. This solution appears clear instead of yellowish. But I personally prefer the DC solution, (I'm just nostalgic that way). I make it in small batches, 1 gallon or less, in order to maintain better consistency of particle size and PPM.

I also came-up with a second use for the pharmaceutical grade water. I'm mixing it with the best MSM on the market and selling that too. MSM has a ton of uses and benefits. I don't have the time to go into it now but, whether used alone or in combination with the colloidal silver, it's a powerhouse. And, more importantly, the shit sells!

There are thousands and thousands of ounces of silver in here; a couple hundred pounds of MSM; and a continuous flow of pure water. It's enough to make hundreds of thousands of bottles of product. Make, sell, reinvest, repeat. What's next? Who knows? Maybe colloidal silver gummies?

CHAPTER TWO:

CONVERSIONS

[The next morning, Gem is awakened by his phone vibrating. He's lying in bed, head still on the pillow, watching his phone dance around on the nightstand.]

Who the fuck is blowing-up my phone at... 6:45 in the morning? Jesus Christ! Who's even up this early on a Saturday?

[Gem hears the boys playing on their tablets.]

They're up already? During the week, you got to do everything but pour cold water over them, to get them out of bed. But on a Saturday, waking up early, not a problem. Oh well, may as well get up, feed the boys breakfast and find out who thinks it's okay to call people this early on a Saturday.

[Gem sits up in his bed and reaches for his phone. He checks his voice-mail, then jumps up in excitement.]

Gem - "Yes! Yes!"

Natasha - "What's going on?"

Gem - "Oh, sorry. Did I wake you?"

Natasha - "Yes…and as loud as you were yelling, you probably woke the neighbors too."

Gem - "Sorry sweetie, I didn't mean to wake you."

Natasha - "Good. I'm going back to sleep."

Gem - "But..."

[Natasha looks at Gem. She wants to go back to sleep but, knows that he's too excited for that to happen.]

Natasha - "Okay...what?"

Gem - "I just got a call from my distributor."

Natasha - "Did he finally get someone to buy your silver stuff?"

Gem - "Oh yeah! Apparently, the reason it's been taking so long, was because a lot of these guys sent the solution out for independent lab testing..."

[Gem staring at Natasha with a huge, excited smile on his face.]

Natasha - "And?"

Gem - "And not only did it test right, it tested so right, that he got me orders for twelve new accounts!"

Natasha - "Twelve?"

Gem - "Yeah baby! Zero to twelve in one phone call. Oh...and most of these guys aren't of the one store variety, this fuckin' guy got us in with several regional chains and two national chains. It's almost eighteen-hundred stores in total!"

Natasha - "Holy-shit!"

Gem - "Holy-shit, is right!"

Natasha - "How big is the order?"

Gem - "You ready?...In total, in different sizes and ppm's...sixteen-thousand bottles!"

Natasha - "Oh my God!"

Gem - "I told you, if you make it right and promote it right, the shit will sell."

Natasha - "What are we going to make off this?"

Gem - "Enough to cover the lab and maybe even have a bit left over, for some more of the shiny stuff."

Natasha - "Are you going to be able to handle it?"

Gem - "Well, the first delivery is for ten-thousand bottles and it's due in three weeks. That's about five hundred bottles per day. Shit! I'm gonna to have to make some adjustments."

[Gem goes to the kitchen and starts cooking eggs and hot dogs for the kids' breakfast. Thinking of how he's going to fill the order.]

Gem Thinks - "I could set up one massive tank but, then the consistency may be off. Or I could set up a shit-load of the same one-gallon tanks and pound them out that way."

[Gem serves the boys breakfast.]

Gem - "Guys, I gotta run down to the lab. Do you need anything else right now?"

Jeffrey - "Mmmm...I'm okay."

Sammy - "Why are you going to the lab right now?"

Gem - "Oh my God! How did I forget to tell you guys? We got orders for our 'silver water'. And they want to buy a lot of it."

Jeffrey - "Like a lot, a lot?"

Gem - "Like a lot, a lot, a lot!"

Jeffrey - "Wow! That's a lot."

Gem - "Yeah it is!"

[Gem checks the kitchen for anything dangerous.]

Gem - "Okay, you guys hurry-up and eat. I'm gonna go and figure out what we have to do. And when you're done, you can help me set everything up."

Sammy - "What? That's not our chore."

Gem - "You're right, it's not. But, I made you guys partners in this company and if you want to keep it that way, you're going to help."

[Boys look at each other.]

Sammy - "Okay..."

Jeffrey - "Okay..."

Gem - "Great! Glad to hear all that enthusiasm. Now, hurry-up and come downstairs when you're done. We've got a lot of work to do."

[Gem goes to the lab and starts tinkering around. Several hours and several trips to the hardware store later; Gem and the boys standing in front of their creation. New tables / shit-loads of new wires everywhere / one-hundred, one-gallon beakers. They took the silver off the shelves and put it on the floor, to make room for the new setup / wires crossing the room / from the power-control box to each beaker, connected to leads and rods.]

Gem Thinks - "Nice. As dangerous as this may seem, it's the solution to our problem. I didn't feel like moving the shelves around and the equipment and machines shouldn't be moved for calibration purposes. So, this mess, is by necessity. In this house, we (meaning the boys and I), focus on function over aesthetics. Obviously."

[Gem looks over at the boys, they both have their lab coats and goggles on.]

Gem - "Hold-on! You guys look way too cute for me not to take a picture of this."

[Gem gets his phone and snaps two pictures. One of just the boys and one of the three of them together.]

Gem - "Okay, you boys ready?"

Sammy - "Ready."

Jeffrey - "Wait, I have to fix my goggles."..."Ready."

[Gem flips the switch. The capacitor makes a high-pitched sound as it begins to charge.]

I draw power from the capacitor because, it's a more reliable and consistent flow. Plus, this way, if the power goes out, I can still finish the job.

[Five days into the colloidal silver making process.]

It's our 5th day of making colloidal silver. Operations are running smoothly. We are almost eight-hundred bottles ahead of schedule. The shelves look so pretty with all the beakers neatly filling them. The boys look so cute in their little lab coats and goggles. I love that they're enjoying this. And who knows, maybe they'll accidentally learn something.

[Power goes off. Gem and boys head back upstairs to see what's happening.]

Gem Thinks - "Did we just pop a breaker or is this an actual outage?"

Gem - "Come-on guys, let's head back upstairs."

Sammy - "But the battery is still working."

Gem - "I know. But it's too dark down here and that makes it dangerous. And that means, we need to head up. We'll just let the battery-pack finish its job. It'll shut-off when it's out of power."

[The boys head upstairs. Gem checks the fuse box, no popped breakers. He checks the power companies "outage map", from his phone.]

Gem - "Damn it! There are a ton of power outages around us. They say the estimated time for repairs is two days."

Natasha - "With all of the thunderstorms we've had the past few days, I'm surprised it didn't go out sooner. What do you want to do?"

Now, you'd think with all the money I spent on the house and the lab set up, that I would have also invested in a whole-house generator.

Unfortunately, that's not the case. It's not that I didn't think about it, I just didn't get to it yet. Oh well, live and learn.

Gem - "Well, I don't want to hang out here. Without electricity, it's like living in the Stone Age. Let's find a hotel and stay there until the power's back."

[Natasha agrees. They pack some stuff for the next couple of days and go to a hotel.]

****

[Two days later: Gem and family return to the house. They see a power-company truck parked near their house. Gem gets out of the car to speak with one of the linesmen.]

Gem - "How's it going?"

Linesman 1 - "Everything is pretty much done. We're just waiting on a few breakers to finish the job."

Gem - "When do you think you'll get them?"

Linesman 1 - "About an hour, maybe a bit longer. It's lunch time and we're going to have to wait for another delivery truck."

Gem - "Okay, thank you."

[Gem gets back into the car and drives-up to the house. They go in and inspect the premises. Everything seems to be in order. Gem goes downstairs to check on the lab.]

Oh, fuck. It's all flooded. There must be four feet of water down here. I guess that's what happens when you have five days of heavy rain, live downhill from your neighbors and don't have a backup for your sump-pump. Shit! We've got to get to the lab and see if we can salvage anything.

[Gem goes back upstairs for help.]

Gem - "It's all flooded. We've got to get what we can out. Boys! Get your flippers on! It's time to put all those swim lessons and practices to good use."

Natasha - "Gem, are you about to take them swimming in a dark, flooded basement? You don't think that's a little too much, even for you guys?"

Gem - "Tashka please; I've seen them swim 200 yards, without a break. This is like, 50 feet max."

Natasha - "What about all the other crap down there? What if the power comes back on?"

Gem - "They'll be fine. They're small and nimble, we have waterproof flashlights and the linesman said that the power won't be on for at least an hour. We'll be done way before that."

Natasha - "I still don't think this is a good idea."

Gem - "Oh, come-on. First of all, this has to get done. Second, they'll have fun doing it. It's a win/win situation."

Natasha - "Do you boys really want to do this?"

Sammy - "I don't know? It's not really our chore."

Jeffrey - "Are we going to get anything extra for it?"

Gem - "Am I gonna have to remind you two how partnerships work?"

[Boys give Gem a blank stare.]

Gem - "Fine, what do you guys want?"

Sammy - "Two large french-fries…each."

Gem - "Done!"

[Sammy and Jeffrey look at each other, excitedly. They run off to get their swim stuff on.]

Natasha - "Can't you wait till the power comes on? The sump-pump will drain the basement and then you can just walk down there."

Gem - "There's too much water down there. When the power comes on, the setup will start to run and make my silver go into the flood water, just to be drained away. This has to be done now."

Natasha - "Fine. But if anything happens to my boys..."

Gem - "If anything ever happens to them, you won't have to punish me. I'll do it myself."

[Boys come running back with goggles and flippers in hand.]

Gem - "Let's go do this!"

Natasha - "Be careful."

Gem - "Don't worry. We're going to have some fun and take care of business at the same time. It's gonna be like an under-water treasure hunt. We'll be up soon."

Jeffrey - "Yeah mommy, don't worry. We'll be back as soon as we're ready to stop having fun."

[Natasha gives Gem an angry look.]

Gem - "Thanks Jeffrey."

[Jeffrey smiles at Gem and all the boys go downstairs.]

Gem - "Hey guys, once we get into that water, there's no messing around; you have to listen to everything I say."

Sammy - "You're making this less fun already."

[They get to the water-line and shine their flashlights around.]

Sammy - "Hey, our basement looks like a pool."

Gem - "Yeah...except, no peeing in this one. I don't want a repeat of what happened at the water park, last summer. You hear me Jeffrey?"

[Jeffrey starts giggling.]

Jeffrey - "Remember how funny it was, when I told the people that you told me to pee in the pool and then they got mad at you?"

Gem - "I didn't tell you to climb out of the pool and pull your shorts down, to do it."

Sammy - "You didn't tell him not to."

Gem - "What are you, his lawyer?"

[Both the boys laugh.]

Gem - "Alright. Let's do this."

[They get into the water and make their way to the lab.]

Gem Thinks - "It's weird swimming around in a pool full of things that can hurt you. Shit. Maybe having the boys here isn't such a good idea."

[They get to the lab.]

This is fucked! All of the equipment is under water; most of the shelves came down and all the solution we already made, has spilled into the flood-water. Even the thousands of dollars' worth of MSM, dissolved into the water.

Gem - "Guys, it looks like everything we made is in the flood water. When this drains, so will all the money we were going to make."

Sammy - "This sucks."

Gem - "This sucks indeed. But it's okay, we'll figure it out. For now, just grab all the silver you can. Get the stuff we had stacked on the floor. Don't bother with the stuff we had hooked-up, it's probably dissolved away by now. This means that this water is full of silver particles and MSM and that makes it very conductive. And that means, when the power comes back, all the rest will get dissolved too. We have to do this quickly. Okay?"

Sammy - "Okay Papa."

[Sammy goes underwater. Gem turns to Jeffrey. He's filling large beakers with the flood water, closing them with stoppers and placing them on the highest shelf he can reach. He gets a few done before Gem notices.]

Gem - "Jeffrey, what are you doing?"

Jeffrey - "You said that all of our silver is in the water. I'm trying to save it."

Gem - "That's very good thinking, Jeffrey. But for now, leave the water. We can't use it anymore. We need to get our silver because, we can still use that."

Jeffrey - "Okay Papa."

[Jeffrey quickly fills a couple more beakers when Gem turns away, then dives under the water. Natasha is upstairs, loading the washing machine for when the power comes back on. Outside, the linesmen get the breakers they need from another utility truck, that was passing by. They insert the new breakers and flip the switch. Natasha sees the lights go on, on the washing machine. She realizes what's happening.]

Natasha - "Oh shit. Gem! Gem!"

[Gem hears the high-pitched sound of the ultra-capacitor batteries charging.]

Gem Thinks - "What the fuck?!"

[He looks over at the battery stack and sees it's almost at capacity / he knows it's about the discharge.]

Gem Screams - "Nooooo!!!"

[He tries to push the boys away. He's too late. A bolt of electricity shoots into Gem, then through Sammy, then Jeffrey and then, blast! Neon blue light fills the water. Gem and the boys are being electrocuted. The entire room turns into a glowing blue, as the ultra-capacitor batteries continue to discharge through the water, causing all the silver in the room to start dispersing. The battery runs out of juice. It's recharging. Gem's and the boys' bodies are floating in the water. Zap! Another discharge from the battery. Natasha gets to the basement door and sees what's happening. She runs out to tell the utility workers to shut the power off. She runs back into the house. The workers follow her in, they see that she's panicking. Natasha runs to the basement. She stops a few steps down, at the water line. She frantically calls-out for Gem and the boys.]

Natasha Crying and Screaming - "Samuel! Jeffrey! Gem!"

[No answer. She sees their bodies floating past her. She reaches into the water to try to pull them out. The high-pitched sound coming from the capacitor again. It's almost recharged.]

Linesman 2 - "What's that noise?"

Linesman 1 - "It sounds like a camera flash charging. Did you turn off the...?"

[Zap! Another shock. This one is the strongest one yet because, of all the conductive material in the water now. Natasha gets thrown back. The linesmen take her back to the kitchen. She's passed out. Her arms look like they've been coded in metal. One of the linesmen runs outside to turn off the distribution box. The other worker checking on Natasha and calling 911. Natasha comes to.]

Natasha - "Please...help my boys."

[The other linesman returns. They leave Natasha and go back to the basement. The blue glow is gone. The high-pitched whistling has stopped. They see Sammy first. Pull out his limp body. Place him on the floor, next to Natasha. His entire body has metal burned into it. One of the linesmen stays with Sammy, to give him chest compressions, the other goes back to retrieve Jeffrey. He lays Jeffery by Sammy, his body like Sammy's; limp, metal burned into everywhere. He wants to go back for Gem.]

Natasha - "No. Take care of him. The kids come first."

[She starts to cry.]

Natasha - "Gem...what did you do?"

[She passes out again. The linesmen look at each other, then continue giving the boys chest compressions. Paramedics arrive. They take over on the boys. Others run down to get Gem's body. They pull him out. He's lifeless. Entire body charred by molten metal. They get him up the stairs, he's unusually heavy. They lay him by the others. The boys already spit-up water and are breathing on their own but, they are still unconscious. The paramedics turn Gem on his side to get the water out of his lungs, then start chest compressions. Gem spits-up water than starts to breathe on his own. He's still unconscious. Paramedics get everyone into ambulances and race to the hospital.]

CHAPTER THREE:

RUDE AWAKENINGS

[Gem blinks his eyes open to a sunlit hospital room. He checks himself for damage. He hears voices, then looks to see Natasha standing by the doorway, speaking with a doctor.]

Gem Thinks - "Shit. What the hell happened last night? Last thing I remember was swimming in the lab... Oh my God, the boys!"

Gem - "Excuse me!"

[Natasha and the doctor both look over at Gem. Natasha runs over to him and starts to kiss him.]

Natasha - "Gem! I'm so happy you're back!"

Gem - "What the hell happened last night? And more importantly, please tell me that the boys are fine and they're at home playing on some screen."

[Natasha looks at the doctor.]

Doctor - "Hello Gem, I'm Doctor Goldman. Your children are in stable condition."

Gem - "Stable condition?! What are you saying? What happened in the lab?!"

Doctor Goldman - "Gem, please relax, you shouldn't be getting too excited right now."

Gem - "Oh, I'm sorry. Did I go over the excitement limit? Well, if you think that not telling me will make me less excited, then you obviously don't fucking know me. Because, not only am I super fucking excited right now but, I'm also getting anxious and annoyed. Which will soon lead to me being pissed-the-fuck-off."

[Natasha looks over at the doctor and nods. He takes the cue and leaves the room.]

Natasha - "Gem, please, just relax. I'm going to tell you everything but, I need you to stay calm. I already thought I've lost you twice and I don't want to go through that again."

Gem - "What? Twice?"

Natasha - "Gem."

Gem - "Okay, sorry. I'm listening."

Natasha - "What do you remember about the night you and the boys went on a recovery mission for your silver?"

Gem - "I remember the basement was totally flooded. We swam into the lab. I remember...oh my God! The battery-stack! Where are the boys?!"

Natasha - "You and the boys were shocked, several times. I tried to pull you guys out but, I was shocked too."

[Natasha begins to cry.]

Natasha - "When they pulled your bodies out...you were limp, lifeless. You were all entirely covered in a charred, metallic substance. As if you were burned by molten metal. And it wasn't just on the skin, it was inside your mouths, eyes, noses, internal organs...everywhere. The doctor said it was probably all the silver particles that attached and later fused with your bodies, after the subsequent electric shocks."

[Gem looks at his hands, arms. Looks at Natasha's hands too.]

Gem - "How did they get it all off?"

Natasha - "They didn't. It just went away after a few days."

Gem - "What? It just fell off my organs?"

Natasha - "No, it just went away. No pieces, not even a flake of it left."

Gem - "What'd I do, absorb it?"

Natasha - "No-one knows. They tried running scans on you but, they ran into problems, your body kept having some sort of reactions."

Gem - "What sort of 'reactions'?"

Natasha - "They said they didn't know."

Gem - "Huh...sounds like they've been saying that a lot. What else don't they know?"

Natasha - "Well...they don't know why you went into cardiac arrest last night."

Gem - "I did what last night? I had a heart attack? What the fuck? Was it something I ate? Bad mix of meds, or something?"

Natasha - "They checked the medical records and didn't find anything that could have caused it."

Gem - "How about a tox-screen? Maybe something they gave me was mislabeled?"

Natasha - "They ran a tox-screen but, the results and the sample got 'misplaced'."

Gem - "How convenient."

Natasha - "And, as far as it being something you ate...you haven't had any real food since you got here. You've been in a coma and getting all of your nourishment through an IV."

Gem - "Coma? How long have I been out for?"

Natasha - "Almost three months now."

Gem - "What the fuck?! Three months?! Natasha, where are the boys? I have to see them, now."

Natasha - "They're on a different floor."

Gem - "What? They're still here?!"

[Natasha starts to cry again.]

Natasha - "You've all been in a coma since that day."

Gem - "Oh my God...I am so sorry. I can't imagine what I've put you through. But now, I have to see my boys."

[Gem stands up and starts pulling all the tubes and wires off of him.]

Natasha - "You probably shouldn't be doing that."

Gem - "When has that stopped me before? Besides, it's okay. I feel good."

Natasha - "Yeah?"

Gem - "Yeah. It's kindda odd but, I feel strong. Like a new me."

Natasha - "A more responsible you?"

Gem - "I think it's cute how you still think that's possible."

[Natasha leads Gem to the boys' room. Gem is taken aback by what he sees. Tubes and wires running in and out of their little bodies. He kneels between their beds, head bowed, tears in his eyes.]

As I look at their little bodies lying there, with wires and tubes sticking in and out of them, I can't help but wonder, what the fuck was I thinking? What the fuck am I always thinking when I come up with these insane ideas? I really fucked-up this time. How do I fix this? Can I fix this? This is the dumbest thing I've ever done, and that's saying a lot, coming from a guy who thrives on doing stupid shit.

Gem - "How bad is it?"

Natasha - "They're in the same state that you were in. It's as if everything is fine but, they just can't wake up."

[Gem stands up, kisses both the boys on their foreheads.]

Gem - "I can't stay here like this. I have to do something. I have to fix this."

Natasha - "Gem, there's something else. I really don't want to bring this up but, I know you'll be pissed if I don't."

Gem - "What's that?"

Natasha - "Um...we're out of money."

Gem - "What? Richard-head hasn't been paying us? Why?"

Natasha - "He said that there was a clause in your contract that allowed him to terminate you, without a severance, if you became legally incapacitated for a period of 14 days or more."

Gem Thinks - "That mother-fucker! What kind of dick does that to someone in a coma? His mom was really onto something when she named him Richard."

Gem - "What about our savings, retirement plans...all my silver?"

Natasha - "I had to cash out of all the savings and sell what little silver was left to pay for all the damage to the house. The insurance company wouldn't cover it because of the lab setup. They said we needed a special rider for that. Add to that, the deductibles and co-pays here, and the regular bills..."

Gem - "Did you call Victor?"

Natasha - "No, I didn't have to. He somehow found out you were here the day after the incident. He's been here at least once a day ever since."

Gem - "That's nice. I meant about money."

Natasha - "He offers it every time he sees me. He even brought a duffel bag full of cash a couple of times. I just didn't feel right taking it without going through you, unless I absolutely had to."

Gem - "I'll take care of it. What else?"

Natasha - "I think that's it."

Gem - "Okay. I'm gonna go and fix what I can."

Natasha - "You just woke up from a coma."

Gem - "Sweetie, if I don't start moving to fix this, the guilt, anger and desperation will eat away at me, until I'm useless. Please, let me fix what I can and at the same time, try to find a way to fix my boys. Besides, I told you, physically I feel great, strong. I don't know, maybe it's because I'm finally well-rested."

[Gem goes to do his check-out paperwork. Physician assistant comes to speak with him.]

Physician Assistant - "Mr. Simonov..."

Gem - "Just Gem, doc."

Physician Assistant - "Mr. Gem, my name is Felix Mendelson. I'm one of the people assigned to your extraordinary case. Before you leave, I'd like to see if we could at least get an MRI of you. We've had trouble trying to scan you and your sons, ever since you were brought in."

Gem - "Yeah, my wife mentioned that. What was the problem?"

Mendelson - "Well, we're not sure. All we know is that your bodies would shake, heat up, move and a whole host of other issues. We didn't want to keep trying, in fear that we may cause irreversible damage to your systems."

Gem - "You know, all this stuff you're saying about 'irreversible damage', really isn't helping sell me on the idea."

Mendelson - "Let me put it this way. Now that you are awake, you can communicate to us, how you're feeling during the procedure. That will provide us with more insight on what's happening to you. If you say 'stop', we stop. If you say you're okay, we continue. I believe it's very important that you do this. What we may learn can help us better understand what has happened to you. And, more importantly, it may help us understand how to help your sons and get them out of their current state."

Gem Thinks - "Ohhh, this mother-fucker's good. He's playing the guilt card, right on the opening hand."

Gem - "Fine. If you think it can help my boys, I'll do it."

Mendelson - "Thank you, Mr. Gem. I think you've made the right decision."

[Gem, Mendelson and an MRI tech, meet in the MRI room. Gem's on the table talking to Mendelson over the intercom, about to be placed into the MRI machine.]

Mendelson - "How are you doing in there?"

Gem - "I'm ready when you are."

Mendelson - "We are about to start the scan. If you feel any discomfort, please let us know immediately."

Gem - "Will do."

Gem Thinks - "Jesus! The way this guy is carrying on, you'd think that he was sliding me into a lion's den. What does he think is going to happen to me? Wait! What does he think will happen to me? Ah, fuck it. Guess I'm about to find out."

[MRI tech starts the machine and Gem begins to slide in on the table.]

Gem - "Um...I'm feeling really warm and some pressure, all around my body. Like someone is trying to push me out of here."

Mendelson - "Are you experiencing any pain?"

Gem - "Not so much pain, just the pressure. And it feels like it's getting stronger. It's building up all around me..."

[Blast of neon blue light as Gem's body shoots out of the MRI chamber with a bang and smashes halfway through the opposite wall. Mendelson and the MRI tech run out to inspect Gem.]

Gem - "Ouch! I hope you got what you needed. Cause, I think we're done here."

Mendelson - "Yes, I think you're right."

[Gem finishes-up with Mendelson and goes to see Natasha before he leaves the hospital. He tells her what just happened during the MRI.]

Gem - "...and there I was, laying there, upper half still in the room; lower half, through the wall and into the hallway. It was crazy."

Natasha - "Oh my God, are you hurt?"

Gem - "No. Surprisingly, I'm okay. I mean, I felt a hard thump but, no pain really."

Natasha - "Huh..."

Gem - "Huh, indeed. Do you have your car here?"

Natasha - "Yes. I used the valet. Let me get you the ticket. Oh, and here's your phone. I've kept it on because Victor asked me to. I think he likes seeing your name when he calls. This ordeal has been surprisingly difficult for him. You should call him. I'll call our families and update them too."

[Gem puts his forehead against Natasha's.]

Gem - "Tashka, I know you've been through a lot of shit lately. I can't even imagine how you've felt because of me. It's my turn. I'm gonna go home, get changed, get my job back, get us some money and be back by dinner time. And by then, maybe they'll know something from the MRI."

[Natasha nods her head. Gem kisses and hugs her, then he leaves.]

****

[Gem gets into Natasha's car and calls Victor.]

Victor - "I'm on my way to hospital now, Natasha. Would you like me to bring something for you?"

Gem - "Yes, you commi-dick! A bag full of that capitalist money you've been hoarding!"

Victor - "Gem! Gem! It's fucking you!"

Gem - "Yes, it's fucking me. What about that money?"

Victor - "How much you need, my friend?"

Gem - "Just get some cash together and meet me at my house in a few hours."

Victor - "I go get it now."

Gem - "No. Go to the hospital first, check on Natasha, get her something to eat. I'll call you soon and tell you when to come by the house."

Victor - "Okay Gem... I'm so happy you're finally okay..."

Gem - "Listen! You can kiss my ass later, right now, just do what I said."

Victor - "No problem. I take care of everything."

Gem - "Good. See you soon."

[Gem gets to his house / runs in / showers / shaves / changes clothes / runs out. Gets back in the car and goes to his office. As he walks through the office, everybody's looking at him as if they just saw a ghost.]

Gem Thinks - "Why the fuck are they all looking at me? Is it the three-month coma thing? The fact that I nearly destroyed everything dear to me? Or maybe they think that I'm about to lose it?"

[Gem walks into Richard's office, closes the door and sits across from him, at his desk.]

Gem - "Sorry for the lack of communication the last few months. I was a bit indisposed; due to being in a coma, and all. But now, I'm back and I think you have some explaining to do."

[Richard still staring at Gem in disbelief.]

Gem - "You gonna say something or are we having a starring contest?"

Richard - "Everything we did was within the scope of your contract. How are we supposed to pay a money manager who's not there to manage the money?"

Gem - "Okay. I can see that. But now, I'm back. So, just give me whatever forms I need to sign to regain my position..."

Richard - "I'm afraid I can't do that."

Gem - "And why is that?"

Richard - "Do you remember that trading algorithm? The one that Tommy was working on for you?"

Gem - "You replaced me with MY algorithm?!"

Richard - "Well, it's been performing, as expected. And since we don't have to give it a cut of the management fee, we've been able to lower the fee structure and attract even more clients to the style. And best of all, I don't have to put up with your insubordination anymore."

Gem - "You know, it's my insubordination that made you money. If it weren't for me, you'd still be running index funds that barely even match their benchmarks and charging such a low fee, that the back-office expenses would eat-up any profits."

Richard - "Be that as it may, you're still out."

Gem - "That algorithm was never meant to be a stand-alone system. It needs tweaking. Otherwise, it will over adjust until it spirals out of control."

Richard - "We'll take care of that if and when it's necessary."

Gem - "What kind of asshole does this to someone in my situation?"

Richard - "The kind of asshole who's sick of dealing with your shit."

At any other time, that's the kind of shit that would get someone thrown through a window. But not today. Because today, I can't afford to let my anger cost me even more, than my irresponsibility already has.

[Gem walks out of the building. Frustrated. Looking up at the heavens. Tommy comes running out after him.]

Tommy - "Mr. Gem! Mr. Gem!"

Gem Thinks - "What, did I forget my balls inside?"

Tommy - "Mr. Gem, I am so sorry for everything. I am sorry for what happened to you and your family. I am sorry that I made that stupid program and I am so sorry you lost your job."

Gem - "Tommy, what happened to my family, was because of me. You writing that software, also me. Me getting fired…mostly because of a dick head, and a little because of me."

Gem Thinks - "Shit! I'm starting to see a pattern here."

Tommy - "I am going to quit! I will not work for a man, like that one."

Gem - "If you quit now, there will be no-one here to make the necessary adjustments to the software. Don't stay for the dick-head. Stay for the clients, who will no-doubt get fucked if you're not here."

Tommy - "You're right, Mr. Gem. I owe it to them."

Gem - "I'll figure something out, Tommy. And when I do, I'll come get you and all of my clients, out of here. Deal?"

Tommy - "Deal."

[They shake hands. Tommy hugs Gem. Gem drives off. As he's driving and thinking of all that has transpired, he starts to get frustrated and angry.]

Gem - "Mother-Fucker!!!"

[He slams his fist against the dashboard. It tears through the center console. Gem stops the car and stares at the damage in disbelief.]

What was that? What just happened? This is either the flimsiest-built car ever or I just did something only a Shaolin Kung-Fu Master should be able to do.

[Gem looks at this hand / not a scratch on it.]

Hmmm, let's try that again.

[Gem raises his fist and hammer-blows the dashboard again / nothing. Again / nothing.]

Oh, I know. I think we need a little more conviction, a little more anger.

Gem - "Mother-Fucker's!!!"

[As Gem's fist is swinging towards the dash / he notices that it's becoming shiny, metallic / SMASH!!! / through the passenger side dash and into the glove-box.]

Okay, good. Now we know that anger works. But what the fuck happened? Did my hand just turn into metal then back again? Let's see how we do with a karate chop?"

[Gem lifts his arm above the passenger seat / takes a few deep breaths / focuses...]

Gem - "Ha-Ya!"

[Sliced right through the seat.]

Well, what do you know? Looks like we just got some wild cards added to this nutty deck. And I'm holding 'em.

[Gem grabs his phone and calls Victor.]

Gem - "Dick, where are you?"

Victor - "I am at my club, getting you money."

Gem - "Okay, grab what you can and hurry the fuck-up."

[Gem hangs up / drives home / walks into the house / walks down to the basement. It's completely refinished. Portable shelves, boxes filled with water damaged things. He walks into the lab and flips-on the lights. It's the only part of the basement that has not been touched.]

It's all toast. The equipment is fried. The silver, drained away. Even the MSM is gone. I can't even look at this place right now. I keep picturing the boys and what must have happened here. You know, I really hope I've learned my lesson this time. But after what I've just discovered in the car, that probably won't be the case.

[Gem turns off the lights and heads back upstairs. He starts looking for things to test his new powers on.]

I think I've had enough of this self-pity, moping around bullshit. Let's see what this new skill is all about. Now, what to destroy?

[Doorbell rings. Gem opens the door. Victor standing there, half-crying, with a duffel bag in each hand. He drops the bags and hugs Gem, as soon as he opens the door.]

Victor - "I am glad to see you, my friend. I thought we lost you."

Gem - "Please Victor, if I die before you, it will throw-off the galactic balance of things. Come-on, we've got a lot of work to do."

[They walk through the house and into the family room. Gem opens the bags and finds one full of hundreds and one full of small bills.]

Gem - "Thanks for this. By-the-way, why the small bills, Vic? You'd better not be selling shit to kids."

Victor - "Don't worry Gem, it's nothing like that."

Gem - "I'm just saying, you know how I feel about that..."

[Gem points to a beaten up, bloody Charlie's Angels lunch box, that's sitting in the clear case on the mantle.]

Victor - "Yes...I know."

Gem - "Besides that; thank you Victor, really, for all your support while I was out and for the money. I'll have it back to you as soon as I can."

Victor - "It's not a loan, it's gift. I owe you everything and I'm happy to have the opportunity to finally give you something back. You saved me. I will always owe you for that."

Gem - "Dude, seriously, if you start crying again, I'm going to have to ask you to leave. And I'm pretty sure you're gonna want to see what I recently discovered."

Victor - "What's that?"

Gem - "Come and see."

[Gem leads Victor out to the garage and shows him the damage in Natasha's car.]

Victor - "Jesus, Gem...what the fuck happen here?"

Gem - "I 'the fuck happen here'."

Victor - "My friend, I know you are pissed about all that is happening. But you don't have to break car...how you even do this?"

Gem - "Well, the first one was by accident. I was hitting the dash out of frustration and...ta-da!"

[Victor staring at Gem with a confused look on his face.]

Gem - "Allow me to demonstrate. Get in."

[Gem gets into the car. Victor hesitates for a minute / Gem waves him in / he nervously gets in.]

Gem - "Watch this. And pay close attention to my hand."

[Gem takes a deep breath / lifts his arm / and goes for another karate chop.]

Gem - "Ha-Ya!!!"

[Gem swings his arm down / it transforms into a metallic ax / splits what's left of the center console. Victor's mouth drops, then turns into a big grin.]

Gem - "Huh...?"

Victor - "That was fucking incredible! I fucking love it! How you do it?"

Gem - "As far as I can tell, so far; I focus on something, think of what I want to do, shape my hand and go through the motion. The rest, just happens by itself."

Victor - "Amazing! What metal is it?"

Gem - "Uh, after what happened, I'm pretty sure it's silver. What else could it be? Now, watch this."

[Gem raises his arm / shapes his hand into a fist / takes a deep breath...]

Gem - "It's hammer time!"

[He throws his arm down / it turns into a metallic sledgehammer / smashes through what's left of the dashboard.]

Gem - "Pretty fuckin' sweet, huh?"

Victor - "What else can you do? Can you do it with other parts of your body? And can you do it without yelling stupid-shit every time?"

Gem - "The answer to all is, I don't know. This is as far as I got so far."

Victor - "Gem, you have fucking super-hero powers. I can't believe this! What was God thinking? This is too much responsibility for a crazy Gemini!"

Gem - "I don't know. I'm guessing he finds the irony amusing and he likes things a little crazy, sometimes. Otherwise, why make people at all?"

Victor - "You have a good point."

[Gem and Victor get out of the car.]

Gem - "You got time?"

Victor - "Oh, for this, I make time. What you want to try next?"

Gem - "I don't know, yet. There are so many possibilities with this, I don't know where to start."

[Gem looks at Victor / he's doing something on his phone.]

Gem - "Dude! Are you even paying attention? What are you doing playing on your phone?"

Victor - "I have idea. I'm looking for super-heroes with same or similar powers. We see what they do, then you try."

Gem - "You don't think it's a little weird to try to figure out this awesomeness, using a bunch of fictional characters?"

Victor - "No, not weird, smart. Why reinvent the wheel? We don't live in a separate universe; it's all been done before. From first recorded writings, people think of super powers. Mythology, ancient Hindu Vedas; even in Holy Bible, there are super powers. Only in Bible powers come from God, not lucky-stupidity like in your case."

Gem - "Alright, what did you find?"

Victor - "I am looking-up heroes who are made from metal. To see if they can do what you can do. Then, we see if you can do what they can do. Okay, first we start with Colossus."

Gem - "Really? Because of his metal powers or because he reminds you of another mother-Russia loving, heavy accent speaking, commi- expat.?"

Victor - "His powers are...very strong, indestructible, good fighter..."

Gem - "Yeah, that doesn't really help me; next."

Victor - "Okay...oh, here... Silver Surfer. He can go through walls, shoot energy, heal people..."

Gem - "Sounds too advanced; next."

Victor - "Let me see...this guy is only metal suit, again metal suit, again metal suit...oh, maybe these guys, Metal Men. Wait, no, just metal robots..."

Gem - "Let me see that phone."

[Gem takes Victor's phone and searches for metal superheroes that can morph.]

Gem - "Here, flip through these. I'm gonna get some batteries and check how conductive I am."

Victor - "Oh, here you go, Mercury...she can shape-shift her body, cling to surfaces, flow like liquid metal...fly..."

Gem - "That's great! Can she shoot lightning out of her ass too?"

Victor - "It doesn't say...but, she does not need to eat or drink."

Gem - "Wow! This chic is starting to sound more and more like that dude from the Terminator 2 movie."

Victor - "Who, Terminator?"

Gem - "No, you boater, the other guy. What the fuck was he called?"

[Victor is looking up.]

Victor - "T-1000?"

Gem - "Yes! Thank you! The T-1000. That guy was awesome."

Victor - "What can he do?"

Gem - "YouTube him. I'm going to try-out the electrical flow thing."

Victor - "Be careful, for Mercury, it said that electricity can hurt her."

Gem - "Dude, I'm not hooking a car battery up to my nipples here, just a couple of 9-volt batteries and an LED bulb. If this works, then we up the juice."

[Gem places his fingers on the batteries contacts / touches the LED with his thumb / the bulb lights up.]

Gem - "We have ignition."

Victor - "You feel anything? "

Gem - "No. Nothing."

Victor - "What next, car battery on nipples or right to wall outlet to ball-sack?"

Gem - "As fun as both those sound, I have a better idea."

[Gem goes out to the garage and comes back with a multimeter. Then he gets a new 9 volt battery, out of the kitchen drawer. He measures the output of the battery.]

Gem - "8.98 volts. Now, let's see how much of it actually gets through."

[Gem, with his left hand, places one finger on each of the batteries terminals / sticks out his right hand / Victor touches the multimeter leads to two of Gem's fingers / then his hand, arm, forehead.]

Victor - "8.95. Everywhere is same. Give me battery; 8.97. That means tiny amount is getting lost or maybe trapped inside you. Huh, maybe you can charge-up too. You know, store some energy, like battery. What if you try with metal hands?"

[Gem takes a deep breath, grunts and flicks his wrists at the same time. His hands turn silver and his fingers extend out several inches / they look like spikes. Victor does 'the cross-thing' and then looks up.]

Gem - "What was that for? What, you think I'm possessed?

Victor - "No. I was thanking God for not giving you this, before we become friends."

Gem - "Oh God! Not that fuckin' story again! Just test me."

Victor - "8.96 you...8.96 battery."

[Victor checks Gem's arms and forehead again.]

Victor - "8.94. Same difference as hands, before turning to metal. Can you turn other parts to metal? Maybe then, more energy get through."

Gem - "I haven't really tried the other parts yet. But I don't see why not."

[Gem closes his eyes, takes a deep breath and grunts. His face and body turn metallic for a second, then back to normal.]

Gem Thinks - "Just as I thought. This shit's everywhere. This is getting awesomer by the minute. Now, I just have to find a way to make it stay."

Victor - "You were all shiny for a second and then back to yourself."

Gem - "I think we'd better work on one body part at a time, until I get used to it. I already have much more control of my hands than I did an hour ago."

[Gem starts to look around.]

Gem - "I gotta find something to kick."

Victor - "Hey, why not kick the car? It's already totaled."

Gem - "Good idea."

[They go back into the garage. Gem kicks the back door and smashes it onto the back seat.]

Gem - "Do you have somebody that can clean this up for me? I really need to get some aggression out."

Victor - "Sure, my friend. I take care of it. You do what you need to do."

[Gem smiles and goes to town on the car, till it's basically a frame with wheels. Gem was able to transform and use every body part he tried.

After the anger management session, they both stand there, looking at the mess, as pieces continue to fall off of the demolished vehicle.]

Gem - "That was nice. I feel refreshed, relaxed."

[Another piece falls off the car and hits the floor with a bang.]

Gem - "Make sure you take care of this. If Natasha sees it, she'll think I'm crazy."

Victor - "What? Afraid she'll find out truth about your crazy-ass?"

Gem - "Suck-a-dick, Victoria!"

[Gem checks the time on his phone.]

Gem - "Shit. I gotta go soon. I promised Natasha I'd be back by dinner. Quick, let's try one more thing."

[Gem runs back into the house. Victor follows. Gem hands him the multimeter.]

Gem - "Here, hold this and stand over there, by the dimmer switch."

[Gem gets on a chair / unscrews a light bulb / makes himself silver and sticks his hand in the socket.]

Gem - "Okay, Give me some juice."

Victor - "Are you sure about this?"

Gem - "No. But do it anyway."

[Victor slowly turns up the dimmer dial / multimeter showing voltage increases.]

Victor - "You okay?"

Gem - "Yeah, just a tiny tingle."

[Victor turns it up halfway.]

Victor - "Now?"

Gem - "Still a tiny tingle. Like it's just passing right through. Step back a little. I want to see if I can hold it and build it."

[Victor moves away / Gem puts his arm across his chest, legs together, head tilted down. He begins to start glowing a faint electric blue color.]

Gem Thinks - "It's working. I can feel the raw energy building-up inside me. I feel powerful. This is so awes..."

[Gem's body flashes a bright, neon-blue / fuse pops / lights go out.]

Victor - "You okay?"

Gem - "Yeah."

Victor - "What happened?"

Gem - "I arched. I got over-energized and then discharged."

Victor - "Did it hurt?"

Gem - "No...more like a release."

Victor - "What, like..."

[Victor makes jerking-off motion.]

Gem - "Kindda but, different. Hey, what'd it say about that chick shooting lightning out of her ass?"

Victor - "It didn't say."

Gem - "That's too bad. 'Cause, that would have been some really useful information, right about now. Hey, remember when Rocky's trainer Mickey told him something about eating lightning and craping thunder? Well, I almost did that just now; except it wasn't thunder."

[Gem and Victor go to their cars.]

Gem - "Tomorrow morning? Around 10ish?"

Victor - "I wouldn't miss it."

Gem - "See you then and thanks for everything."

Victor - "It's my pleasure."

[They get in their cars and go their separate ways / Gem to the hospital / Victor, who knows where. When Gem gets back to the hospital / back to reality / looking at the reminders of his mistake / at the two little boys laying there in those beds. He hesitates before he enters the room.

Natasha is getting food out of plastic containers, that friends and relatives brought for them. She smiles happily when she sees Gem.]

Natasha - "When I told our moms that you were up, they made all your favorites and brought them for you."

Gem - "Wow! Check out this spread. How was your day? Any news on the boys?"

Natasha - "Same as it's been the past three months. Except now, because you're back, I feel hope again and I don't feel alone anymore."

Gem - "I'm so sorry."

Natasha - "I know you are, Gem."

Gem - "I promise you, no more stupid shit with the kids."

Natasha - "I really wish I could believe you this time."

Gem Thinks - "And I really wish I meant it this time. But who am I kidding? After what I've discovered today, that's highly unlikely."

Natasha - "Come-on, let's eat. I want to hear about your day."

[Gem and Natasha ate dinner. Gem told her about everything that happened that day (minus the car thrashing in the garage) / showed her some of what he can do and they fell asleep together on the couch.]

****

[The next morning, Gem, after having breakfast with Natasha, heads home to meet with Victor. When he gets home, he sees that the car he destroyed has been removed. While he waits for Victor, he YouTube's T-1000 scenes from "Terminator 2: Judgment Day".]

I remember this guy was bad ass. He could do all kinds of sweet shit. They had to melt him in a vat of other molten metals, to stop him. Hmm...I gotta make a mental note of that. In fact, I should start looking up how all these "indestructible superheroes" meet their fates. Then see if I could protect myself from them. Okay,

Number one: stay away from things and places that can melt me.

Number two: acid baths seem to come up a lot in this search; stay away from acid

Number three: energy; well, energy blasts I'm not too worried about, just have to practice it more...

[Doorbell rings / Victor's here / Gem opens the door to find Victor standing there, with another huge duffel bag.]

Gem - "Prevet Veetsok. What's in the bag?"

Victor - "Just some things for testing. Last night, I can't sleep. I watch T-1000 from Terminator movie. I think you are right. This is our guy to start with."

[Victor sets the bag on the counter and opens it up. It's loaded with weapons; high caliber pistols and rifles, blow torch, reciprocating saw...]

Gem - "What the fuck, Vic?!"

Victor - "What? Just things to test stuff from movie."

Gem - "Yeah...and I'm the one with a problem. Why don't we try to emulate his moves first?"

Victor - "Then this?"

Gem - "Then we'll see. You fuckin' sadist."

[Gem and Victor start watching more of the videos to determine what they'll try.]

Victor - "Okay, this one with spike hands, we know you can do. Making metal objects from body, also can do. How far can you stretch? Not just hands; legs, chest, head...everything."

Gem - "How 'bout my dick? You wanna see how far I can stretch that too?"

Victor - "No. You can do that on private time. But I am curious to know results."

Gem - "Pervert."

[Gem and Victor walk out to the backyard. Gem lays on the grass in "starfish" formation and stretches out all his appendages. Victor begins taking measurements.]

Gem - "Let's use this to get our baseline measurements."

Victor - "I think you can do more."

Gem - "I'm sure I can but, I'd have to go thinner and I don't want to overdo it."

Victor - "What if, instead of making thinner, you move more of thicker part to thinner part? Then you make thinner part thicker so you can stretch out more."

Gem - "Victor, you lost me at 'what if'. Can you please just measure this so, we can move on to something a little more interesting? I promise, I'll try whatever it is you just said, later."

I understood what he said. You don't spend your life around boaters with heavy accents and broken English and not understand their dialect. I just want to move on to the fun stuff. Truth be told, I can't wait to get to some of the shit he has in that bag.

Victor - "Okay. Legs about 6 feet each, arms about 4 feet each, head...hard to measure because, it's growing by the minute."

Gem - "Save the color commentary, will ya?"

Victor - "Okay, now; electricity, we have starting-point and blow-up point. Stretching, basically every part double...without even trying. "

[Victor gives Gem a dirty look.]

Gem - "We need to test thermal tolerances and conductivity."

[Victor pulls a blowtorch out of his bag. With a big smile on his face.]

Gem - "You know, it's a little concerning for me, to see you pull that out with such a smile on your face."

Victor - "I haven't used these tools since KGB days. They bring back many memories."

Told you he was a sadistic fucker.

Gem - "Just light the bitch."

[Victor lights the blowtorch / Gem quickly moves his hand across the flame's path / nothing. He slows his movements until, his hand stops right above the flame. With Victor's infrared thermometer, Gem measures the temperature at the bottom of the hand, where the flame is hitting. At 993 degrees Fahrenheit, it feels warm. He measures the other side of his hand; at 969 degrees Fahrenheit, it's conducting well. Next, Victor pulls out a large, metal, meat tenderizing mallet.]

Victor - "Now, we test impact and pressure resistance."

[Victor hits Gem's hand with the mallet, lightly.]

Victor - "Anything?"

Gem - "I can feel it but, it doesn't hurt."

[Victor takes a full swing and hits Gem's hand again.]

Gem - "Nope."

[Victor hits Gem in the chest, back, face; harder and faster; until he's out of breath.]

Gem - "Same. Still feeling some pressure, still no pain."

Victor - "No brain, no pain."

Gem - "That's real cute; can we move on?"

[Victor pulls-out a pointy, metal spike and a pair of bolt cutters.]

Victor - "Now we check puncture and cut resistance."

[Victor places the spike on Gem's left hand and taps it lightly with the mallet.]

Victor - "Okay?"

Gem - "Same shit, different torture device."

[Victor raises the mallet and hits the spike, full force. It punctures through Gem's hand and comes out of the other side.]

Gem Screams - "Ahhhhh...oh my God! That fucking hurts!"

[Victor scrambles to pull the spike out.]

Victor - "Sorry. Sorry, my friend."

Gem - "I'm just kidding. I'm okay. I feel it but, still doesn't hurt."

[Victor yanks the spike out. They stare at Gem's hand in disbelief, as they watch the hole heal itself.]

Gem - "Hmmm...good to know."

[Victor takes the bolt cutters and snips Gem's left pinkie off.]

Gem - "What the fuck, Vic?!"

Victor - "Sorry, I'm just very excited. Did it hurt?"

Gem - "No. But now what?"

[Victor picks-up Gem's severed finger and looks at it for a second. It's all silver. Can't see bones or flesh.]

Victor - "Let me try something."

[Victor lines-up Gem's finger to his hand.]

Victor - "If hole reconnects to close, maybe this also reconnects."

Gem - "You better hope it does."

[Victor touches the severed finger to Gem's hand. They watch in amazement as the finger reattaches and Gem regains full range of motion.]

Gem - "Hmmm...good to know. Hey Victor, I know you're excited but, can you settle down a bit? The next thing you do, may not fix itself so easy. Okay?"

Victor - "Okay, okay, I'm sorry."

[Victor looks back in the bag.]

Victor - "Next step is to test armor and healing."

[Victor pulls-out a 50 caliber, short-barrel rifle.]

Gem - "God damn it! Did you not hear me? Put that fucking cannon away! Jesus!...Besides, this is a residential area. Do you want these people calling the cops?"

Victor - "If spike go through hand, no pain and cutting off finger, no pain and then both heal...then what is big deal about bullet? Makes same hole only faster. Look, you have big property with fence and trees, nobody will see shit. And don't worry about noise, I have sound suppressor."

Is it bad that what this trained manipulator is saying is making sense to me? I mean, only an idiot would try something like this at this point in the game, right?

Victor - "It's okay Gem, I understand. Family life has made my fierce-fighting friend, into little pussy."

Is it bad, that I'm about to get shot, just to prove this funky-boater wrong?

Gem - "Fine, you asshole! Just not in the dick, balls or face."

What the hell am I doing?!

[Victor smiles, devilishly / shoots Gem right in the gut.]

Gem - "Ouch! Really dick?! You couldn't do the leg or something?"

Victor - "Did it hurt?"

Gem - "Just when it went in and again when it came out and a little more in between. But not as bad as you'd think, sort-of like an unexpected hit in the nuts from one of my boys."

Victor - "Let's check damage."

[Gem removes his hand from the entry point. Victor inspects.]

Victor - "Just half-inch entry wound."

[Victor looks at the hole closer and sees it goes all the way through. He walks behind Gem to inspect the exit wound. It's about 4 inches across. The silver is peeled back but, quickly healing.]

Gem - "How's the back?"

Victor - "Uhhh...about same. Let's move to next thing."

Gem - "And what's that? You got a little nuke in there? Maybe shove it up my ass and see what happens?"

Victor - "No. We try becoming like liquid metal, thing. You know, when T-1000 melts-up from floor or when he walk through jail door, at crazy hospital."

Gem - "That was pretty sweet. Where should we try it?"

[They look around the yard. Victor takes the grate from Gem's grill.]

Victor - "Here. Let's start small. See if you can morph your hand through this."

Gem - "Really? When it came to 'armor testing', you had no problem pulling out the big guns but, this you wanna to take slow? You backwards-ass, mother-fucker."

Victor - "We doing this or you going to cry all day?"

Gem - "Asshole."

Victor - "Fucking Gemini. One minute 'yes', next minute 'no'. I never know what your other side will do next."

Gem - "Don't worry, neither do I. That's what makes it fun."

[Gem places his hand on the grate. He starts to push down slightly but, nothing is happening.]

Gem - "It's not working."

Victor - "It's not working because, you are trying to push through it."

Gem - "What?"

Victor - "Instead of trying to push through, you have to try to morph around it. Try to visualize your hand melting around the bars and coming back together, on other side. Like Bruce Lee said, 'flow like water'."

Gem - "Whatever you say, Sensei."

Victor - "Who's Sensei?"

Shit. I forgot who I was talking to.

Gem - "Never-mind."

[Gem closes his eyes and imagines his hand flowing through the grate.]

Victor - "You are doing it! See, you crazy bastard."

Gem - "Yes, it's very exciting. You finally got something right. Congratulations! You should mark the date on your calendar."

[Victor looking at Gem standing there in his warm-up pants and, the now, fucked-up t-shirt.]

Victor - "You need costume."

Gem - "For what?"

Victor - "All super-heroes have recognizable costume."

Gem - "You mean a suit?"

Victor - "Yes, suit. So, people recognize who you are but, we make mask so they don't know who you are."

Gem - "Why would I want people to recognize me? Wouldn't it make more sense to go incognito?"

Victor - "When people know you only by suit; when you take suit off, you are even more 'incognito' than before."

Gem - "You manipulative genius. Looks like someone paid attention in KGB class."

Victor - "More than you think. This persona is just an act to throw people off. Makes me more unpredictable."

Gem - "Well, since you've done such a great job acting like a jackass for the past 20 years, you think you could act like a normal person for a little while? You know, mix it up a bit. That would really throw everyone off."

Victor - "Why change it if it's working? Besides, you wouldn't love me any other way."

Gem - "You know what's funny? I think you're right."

[Victor checks his watch / it's almost 1 pm.]

Victor - "I'm hungry. You want to go to my club? I have chef make us nice, fat burgers; like you like."

Gem - "I could eat but, not at the club."

Victor - "Why not my club?"

Gem - "Too many hot chicks at your place. I haven't had sex in months. And I can't afford to spend the rest of the day jerking off."

[They go to the local diner. Sit down and order their food.]

Victor - "Like I was saying, suit is easy. You get one-piece, spandex jogging suit. Then underwear, like briefs only without pee-hole, to put on over jogging suit. But it has to be different color, for contrast."

Gem - "Right, contrast. Because otherwise, it would just look weird."

Victor - "Oh, and cape. You need to have cape."

Gem - "Yeah? What's the cape for? To keep the spandex bodysuit with the underwear pulled over it, from looking stupid? No, I need something simple and easily replaceable. Like the stuff I have on now, with some kind of martial arts or boxing robe thrown over it. That way, it will be easy to get on and off and it'll be loose enough to not tear, every time I stretch."

Victor - "I got it! Robe like death guy!"

Gem - "You mean the Grim Reaper?"

Victor - "Yes but, not as long. Maybe just 3/4 length boxing robe. You get it in black, put on hood and silver mask and maybe that thing he uses to kill people."

Gem - "It's called a scythe. And I'm pretty sure it's used for harvesting souls, not killing people."

Victor - "Same shit. Anyways, we make them shorter and put two of them on back of your suit. Like Deadpool's swords but, yours will be farm tools."

Gem - "I love it! Wow Vic, two in one day. I guess you were due after a 20-year drought."

Victor - "Wait, I have more. You also need to have alias name."

[Their food comes and they start to eat.]

Gem - "Why do I need an alias? I already have one, remember? Gem is not my real name. It's the name you gave me after our little incident, and it stuck. I'm just glad the original 'Fucking Gemini' version didn't stick. That one would have been more difficult to explain at PTA meetings."

Victor - "How about Gemini?"

Gem - "Ooo, I like it. Very creative. Let's search it."

[Gem takes out his phone and does a search for superheroes named Gemini.]

Gem - "There are four of these guys? Talk about a laps in creativity."

Victor - "So, what's one more?"

Gem - "No. How about Silver-something?"

[Gem does a search for superheroes with silver in their name.]

Gem - "We have, the Silver Surfer, Silver Samurai...Quicksilver...Silver Sorceress. Silver this, silver that...none of these fuckers are even made of silver."

Victor - "How about Silver-Gem? You're silver, you're Gem; Silver-Gem."

Gem - "Holy-shit, Vic! That's three today! I'm going to petition Congress to make today Victor Petrov day."

Victor - "So, you like it?"

Gem - "I fucking love it!"

Victor - "Also, you need symbol."

Gem - "Symbol, for what?"

Victor - "What, you gonna write name on suit with silver marker? No. You need a symbol to represent Silver-Gem, something about you. I got it, mask like happy and sad face from drama. Except, for you, we make it half happy, half pissed-off face with nothing in middle. We make it opposing colors, like silver for happy side and red for angry side. It's perfect. The whole thing is like you, always on the edge of the other side."

Gem - "You know, what little of that I understood, I actually like. That makes four for the day. I don't know what you've been doing these past few months but, whatever it is keep doing it. I like this new, not so useless Victor."

[Gem's phone starts to ring. He doesn't recognize the number.]

Victor - "You going to get it?"

Gem - "No. I never pick-up if I don't know who's calling. I'll just let it go to voice-mail. If they need me, they can leave a message."

[They continue eating. Gem's phone chimes.]

Gem - "See, they left a message."

[Gem picks-up his phone and listens to the voice-mail.]

Voice-mail - "Hello Mr. Gem, this is Wilhelm Dietrich from Lockhart Industries. Please call me back at this number, at your earliest convenience. This is a matter of great importance. Thank you."

Gem - "It's that douche-bag that took over Lockhart."

Victor - "What does he want? "

Gem - "He wants me to call him back. Didn't say why but, apparently it's 'a matter of great importance'."

Victor - "You going to call him?"

Gem - "Fuck him. If it's that important, he can call again. He's not even worth me hitting redial."

Victor - "Who is he?"

Gem - "Wilhelm Dietrich, a sleazy, shit-bag of a man. I wouldn't trust him for anything. Hey Vic, why don't you see if you can get some intel on this guy?"

Victor - "I call my people. Give me few days. Tomorrow is weekend, everybody out."

Gem - "When you can."

[Victor drops money on the table for the bill. They go back to Gem's house. Gem gets out of the car, Victor stays in.]

Victor - "I have to get back to Club. Friday night, you know."

Gem - "Go do what you need to do. I'm gonna do a couple of things around here, then go back to the hospital."

Victor - "And Gem, remember; it's not how you get powers or what powers you have, it's what you do with them that make you different. You are a good-hearted man with an over-developed sense of justice, you will fit right in with rest of those crazy-asses."

Gem - "Thanks. And Victor, thank you for being awesome."

[Victor looks back at Gem like he's about to cry.]

Victor - "And thank you for giving me my life."

Gem - "I didn't 'give' it to you, Vic. I just showed you it was worth keeping. You did the rest. Now get the fuck out of here, before you start to cry and ruin the moment."

[Victor smiles and drives away.]

Victor - "Fucking Gemini."

[Gem heads into the house for the three S's; shit, shower and shave. While he's shaving, he notices a strange glimmer in his eyes.]

Gem Thinks - "What's this?"

[He moves his eyes and head around to figure out where the reflection is coming from. He looks closer into the mirror and sees that it's coming from his eyes. Both pupils have a thin, silver ring around them. He grabs his wife's makeup mirror, for a closer look and discovers that the rings dilate when he turns off the lights. So much so, that you can barely see the whites of the eyes.]

Holy shit-sticks! I can see clear as day. Albeit, without much color. I'm picking up some hues but, nothing vivid. I have to remember to check the boys for this; and Natasha too. How sweet would that be? We'd be one, bad-ass family. Let's keep our fingers crossed for that one.

CHAPTER FOUR:

GETTING BACK TO WORK

[Gem gets dressed, gets in his car and drives back to the hospital. When he gets there, he hesitates, again, before walking into the boys' room. Natasha is not there. He sees her coat, purse and phone on a chair.]

She must have stepped out for a bit. I need to check the boys' eyes before she gets back. I don't want to get her hopes up for nothing.

[Gem looks at his sons laying there, motionless, almost lifeless.]

Every time I see them, I want to punch myself in the face. It sucks without them. I miss everything about them.

[Gem hears Natasha coming / quickly checks the boys' eyes for silver rings / nothing there.]

Fuck! How did they not get this too? They went through exactly the same thing as I did. Did I just get lucky? Or is this an ironic, double-whammy for me being such a dumb-ass?

Natasha - "Hey, Gem."

Gem - "Hey beautiful. Any news?"

Natasha - "Same as before."

Gem - "How are you? Do you need anything?"

Natasha - "Uh...you came out of a three-month coma yesterday and have been running around like crazy. Do you need anything?"

Gem - "Everything I need, is in this room."

[Gem's phone rings / it's Willie again.]

Gem - "Damn it! This guy again? What does he want from me?"

Natasha - "Who is it?"

Gem - "Remember that guy I told you about? The one who screwed John Jr. out of Lockhart?"

Natasha - "The douche-bag"?

Gem - "The one and only."

[Phone stops ringing.]

Natasha - "He must know you're not at your old firm anymore, what do you think he wants?"

[Notification chimes / Gem checks his voice-mail.]

Gem - "Same as last time, 'please call back', 'matter of great importance'. Let me call him back. I have a feeling; he'll just keep stalking me out if I don't."

[Gem walks out of the room and calls Willie back. Comes back a few minutes later.]

Natasha - "What did he say?"

Gem - "It was weird. He was being all nice. He said he knew about my job, and our 'unfortunate incident'. He wants me to meet him for dinner at his country club tonight, to discuss a consulting gig of some sort."

Natasha - "Are you going?"

Gem - "I told him 'yes'."

Natasha - "But you said he's a douche-bag."

Gem - "Yes, that he is. But he's a douche-bag with access to a ton of money. So, let's see what he has to say."

Natasha - "Alright Gem, just don't let this be a repeat of that time-share thing in Mexico. 'Cause, I'm not going to be there to stop it this time."

Gem - "That was funny! Remember how scared those two guys got when you said you'll cut off their balls? I love that story."

[Gem kisses Natasha and the boys and heads out. As he walks through the hallway, he sees a medical box with his name on it. PA Mendelson is standing next to it, speaking with a courier.]

Gem - "Where's my stuff going?"

Mendelson - "Hey there, Gem. I'm sending this over to some colleagues, who are much better equipped to figure out your situation."

Gem - "That's a lot of files."

Mendelson - "Yes, as you can see, we've done a lot to try to figure-out what happened to you and how it's changed you. You are an extraordinary case, Mr. Gem. And now that you're up and about, it is my hope that we can use these files and you, to help bring back your children."

Gem - "If that's the case, you do what you need to do. And, please let me know what I can do to help."

Mendelson - "We certainly will."

[They part ways. Gem goes to Willie's Country Club. When he arrives there, he is seated at Willie's table.]

Willie - "Mr. Gem, thank you for making the time to meet with us on such short notice. This gentleman is Mr. Sauer, he's one of my closest associates."

[Gem and Mr. Sauer shake hands.]

Mr. Sauer - "Sebastian Sauer."

Gem - "Gem."

Willie - "I call him, The Specialist."

Gem - "Yeah? What exactly does he specialize in?"

Willie - "Anything that I may require."

Gem - "Sounds like a good guy to have around."

Willie - "The best! He helps me, by handling our...special projects. Honestly, I don't know where I'd be without him."

Gem - "That's great. So, do you want to tell me what it is you need my help with or was that just a ruse to set me up on a blind date with, Mr. Sauer here?"

Willie - "First off, Mr. Gem, I would like to acknowledge our first meeting. I know I came off as a show-off, trying to belittle you as I was attempting to show strength and dominance. John Jr. tried to warn me not to do it. His exact words to me were, 'pick somewhere else to start, this guy is going to embarrass you'. I thought he was just being bitter about the chairmanship vote. But in hindsight, his warning was sincere."

Gem - "John Jr. is a man of integrity, just like his father was. He knows that company like no-one else. It would be in your best interest, to listen to him."

Willie - "After getting to know him better, I would have to concur with your assessment."

Gem - "Are you apologizing to me right now?"

Willie - "I want our slate clean. This project I have planned, could very well be the most important thing that either of us has ever done."

Gem - "Hold that thought. I need to use the restroom."

[Gem gets up from the table and walks to the bathroom.]

This shit sounds like it's about to get heavy. Guys like that, don't apologize to anyone unless they have an ulterior motive. And this guy, always seems to have an ulterior motive. There is no way in hell I'm gonna let this conversation go on, without recording it. I have a feeling that whatever he's about to tell me will be a half-truth and only the tip of the iceberg, compared to his true intentions.

[Gem finishes up and goes back to the table with his phone's voice recorder on.]

Gem - "Sorry about that. Please, continue."

Willie - "As I was saying, this project is the kind of thing that will get our names into history books. Money, fame, power...control, true greatness."

Gem - "You know, I'm pretty happy staying under the radar. All those things you just mentioned, don't really mean shit to me. The only opinions that matter to me, are those from my friends and family. And they already know how 'truly great' I am. So, why don't you explain what you need from me and we'll take it from there?"

Willie - "Fair enough. It has been brought to my attention, that your accident, the one that should have killed you, may have physically changed you. Do you feel different in anyway?"

Gem - "Yes, I do."

[Willie smiles / thinking Gem is about to open-up.]

Gem - "I feel...poorer, sad, responsible and even a little hornier than usual."

Willie - "I meant physically, not emotionally."

Gem - "Physically, I feel great. Like I can take on the world."

Willie - "That, Mr. Gem, is precisely what I'm talking about."

Gem - "My ego?"

Willie - "No, although that is a bit of a concern for me. What I am referring to, is your newfound abilities."

Gem Thinks - "Oh, shit. What does this guy know?"

Willie - "Allow me to elaborate."

Gem - "Please do."

Willie - "I heard the news of your incident, from your former employer. He called me to tell me, that he was now in the position to give us the pricing we had previously requested."

Gem - "Wait! He voluntarily called you to lower the fee?"

Willy - "Yes."

Gem - "What a dick-head."

Willie - "To be honest with you, those were my sentiments as well."

Gem - "So, what? He told you he fired me because, I was in a coma?"

Willie - "Yes. He said it nullified your contract, and then he proceeded to tell me the story as he knew it and which hospital you were in. Now, contrary to what you may think of me, I am a man of compassion. I went personally to visit you and your family. While there, I spoke with the doctors and they told me everything that happened but, they didn't understand it. Luckily for us, the consortium with which I am affiliated, owns several, top-tier medical research facilities. I told the doctors would be willing to examine your case. They sent us what they had and to my amazement, even our doctors couldn't understand what was happening to you. Then yesterday, I get a call saying that you had checked yourself out of the hospital. At that point, my curiosity got the best of me. So today, I sent a couple of my people to investigate the situation further."

Gem - "You spied on me?"

Willie - "I prefer the term 'investigate' but, I suppose there isn't much difference."

[Willie picks up a tablet computer.]

Gem Thinks - "Shit!"

Willie - "They couldn't believe what they were witnessing."

Gem Thinks - "Oh, fuck. Please don't have me on video."

[Willie turns on a clip of Gem and Victor testing powers.]

Gem - "Wow! That's crazy. Who is that guy? And why is he in my yard?"

Willie - "That guy, appears to be you. And, as far as how and what he's doing; that's what we intend to find out."

This is not good. They only got a little of our two-day session. But what little they got, was big. They have from, right after I got shot, to my hand going through the grate. Pretty important shit. They must have stuck their cameras over the fence, after they heard the gun-shot. Sound suppressor my ass...damn-it Victor.

Willie - "I especially like this part, in the beginning, right after your associate shoots you. Tell me Mr. Gem, do you think it's normal for a man to, not only live but, also quickly heal from such a wound?"

Gem Thinks - "That's what my back looked like? Fucking Victor."

Gem - "Now I remember. My friend is a special effects guy, for movies and such. I was just helping him test some of his gear. Pretty sweet huh?"

[Willie and Gem stare at each other. They both know the truth.]

Willie - "I am prepared to offer you $100,000 for one month of your time and cooperation."

Gem - "For what? To do special effects tricks?"

Willie - "$200,000."

This is getting crazier by the second. $200,000 for one month? That will cover most of what we lost, financially. But I don't trust this guy. Fuck! What to do?"

Willie - "$300,000."

Gem - "No. And it's not the money, it's you. I don't trust you."

Willie - "What assurances would you require of me?"

Gem - "I want to know your motives. Your true motives. And then I'll make my decision."

Willie - "I understand. Perhaps we would do well to take this conversation to a more private venue. My estate is a very short drive from here. We can talk candidly and I will do my best to address any of your concerns. What do you say?"

Gem Thinks - "I really don't want to do this but, at this point, what do I have to lose? He already knows."

Gem - "Okay, Willie. I will give you one hour of my undivided attention. After which, you will respect any decision that I make. Deal?"

Willie - "I couldn't ask for anything more."

[They get into their respective cars and head-out to Willie's estate. Upon arrival, Gem notices that the entire property looks like a construction site. They walk in and go into Willie's study for drinks.]

Willie - "What will it be, Mr. Gem?"

Good question. Of course, my eyes just naturally move straight up to the top shelf. Ohhh, he's got the good stuff.

Gem - "I'll have the cognac."

[The Specialist goes for the cheaper one.]

Gem - "No, not that one...the Louis XIII, on the top shelf."

A nice, unopened bottle. You see, I'm not much of a drinker and even if I were, I wouldn't drink anything that guy is dispensing. But if I'm going to waste something, it may as well be the most expensive thing on the shelf. It's gonna to be the good stuff.

[Willie walks over to a large, old portrait on the wall.]

Willie - "This is my great-grandfather, Wolfgang Dietrich. He was a truly, great man. Came from poverty, amassed a fortune and died a national hero. He put our family on the proverbial 'map'. Since then, the following generations lived well and kept things running but, neither my father nor my grandfather were able to obtain any levels of true, individual accomplishment. Neither left a historic legacy of their own; both regretted it till their dying day. I do not wish to, as they say, 'go out like that'. In fact, I wish to create a legacy for my family, that will give us world-wide notoriety. And that, Mr. Gem, is where you come in."

Gem - "So, let me get this straight, you want to ride my coattails into the history books?"

Willie - "Precisely."

Gem - "Well, I don't see how that's going to work. First of all, I don't want to be famous because, I don't like attention from strangers. Second, the only legacy I care about is my kids."

Willie - "Let's talk about that."

Gem Thinks - "Damn it! Why'd I bring it up?"

Willie - "Money aside, I am a very well-connected man. Best schools, best universities, best placement post-graduation. The sky's the limit. But we have another issue to deal with, before we can deal with those. I think that we may be able to help with that issue, as well. Come with me, I want to show you something."

[Gem follows Willie down to the huge, walkout basement.]

Willie - "I want to show you my level of dedication to this project."

[Lights go on.]

Holy shit! Now this is a lab. Everything you need to poke, cut, scan, magnify and do whatever else with. He even has an electron microscope.

Willie - "I had this built specifically for this project. As you can see, I spared no expense. It will be the same with the researchers, best of the best. It is my hope that the information we discover here, will resolve both of our legacy issues."

Gem - "Wow! How the hell did you get this build so fast?"

Willie - "We have a specialized team. They already built two this week and are in the process of finishing a third for another project or a backup, if we should need one."

Gem - "What else should I know?"

Willie - "We are also building a training course out in the yard. But we'll have to see that another time. It hasn't been completed, and it's getting too dark out to really appreciate it."

Gem - "Let's talk details."

Willie - "Ah, a sign of interest. What are your requests?"

Gem - "I only have one. I put forth the terms of the contract. There will be none of that line-item-veto bullshit. No negotiations. It will be all or nothing, take it or leave it."

Willie - "If that's what you insist. When do you think you can have it ready?"

Gem - "Don't worry, I'll keep it very simple for everybody. Just give me a piece of paper, a pen and a couple of minutes."

[The Specialist provides Gem with paper and pen. As Gem begins to write, he notices The Specialist is trying to look over his shoulder. He moves the paper around but, The Specialist is still trying to look.]

Gem - "Really dude?!"

[The Specialist gets embarrassed. He steps away. Gem finishes the "contract" and hands it to Willie.]

Terms of Contract:

1) Duration 3 weeks - 15 business days only / weekends off / 8AM-4PM

2) Compensation Prior to Work - All payments to be made in cash (US Dollars) and/or gold; prior to expected duties being performed

3) Privacy / Anonymity - neither mine nor my family's names or likenesses are to be shared with or communicated to, anyone

4) There will be no pressure placed on me to do anything I don't want to do

5) I have full control. No test or procedure will be conducted without my expressed permission. I can veto anything that I don't see fit. I decide the depth and scope of everything.

[End of contract]

I wasn't trying to do the "lawyer thing" and create a bunch of ambiguous loopholes. The entire contract was one, big loophole; designed for my benefit and protection, not his.

Willie - "This 'contract' looks extremely one-sided. You don't even specify the amount of the payment."

Gem - "Yeah, if it looks that way, that's because it is. It's designed to protect me from you, not you from me. And as far as the amount goes, it's one-million-dollars and it's just between you and me. Government claw-back rules are a bitch."

Willie - "What assurances do I have that you will live up to your end of the bargain? The way this is written, you are not required to do anything."

Gem - "You know, if you ask around, you'll find a lot of people who don't like me, for one reason or another. Something I said, something I did, maybe someone I hit; but you'll never find anyone who'll say that I cheated them."

Willie - "We did and you are correct, in both regards."

Gem - "And that's only because they don't like the truth and/or don't appreciate poetic justice."

[Willie still looks concerned.]

Gem - "Look, I know the money is not the issue; trust is. Even with all that was shown and said, I still don't trust you, you still don't trust me."

[Gem gets up.]

Gem - "Thank you for dinner and the drink."

[Gem puts out his hand for a goodbye handshake. Willie signs the contract and hands it to Gem.]

Willie - "I have made the first leap of faith."

[Willie hands the pen to Gem.]

Willie - "Would you be willing to do the same?"

[Gem stares at Willie's eyes / he sees his desperation.]

I know I probably shouldn't be doing this but, my curiosity won't let me pass on it. Plus, if I say no, I'm pretty sure that won't be the end of it. This guy is desperate, who knows what he'll do. You know that saying, "keep your friends close but, your enemies closer"? I'm not saying he's an enemy but, from what I know so far, I think he's got a lot of potential. I'll learn more from the inside.

[Gem signs the contract.]

Gem - "There are billions of dollars to be made from beneficial uses of this. If I even suspect you're using this for something remotely sinister, we're done. Understood?"

Willie - "Understood."

Gem - "Great!"

Willie - "Now, how would you like your payment?"

Gem - "What do you have?"

[Willie swings open his great-grandfather's portrait, to reveal a safe in the wall.]

Really?! A safe behind the portrait? How fucking original?! As if he wasn't a bad enough cliche already.

[Willie opens the safe.]

Oh! My! God!!! I thought I had a stash. This fucker's got everything! It's like a huge walk-in closet full of money, gold, silver, gemstones and lots of other expensive shit. And I mean a lot of it. Tens of millions of dollars' worth. He also has a shit-load of what look to be futuristic weapons and guns. I don't know what the fuck those are for but, I would hate to be on the receiving end of one of them. It's obvious he's used to dealing like this. See, I already learned something.

Gem - "I'll take half in those 100-ounce, RCM gold bars and the other half in cash."

Willie - "You don't like the Swiss kilo bars?"

Gem - "The RCM's are a higher quality plus; I don't feel like doing the kilo to troy ounce calculations when I go to sell."

Willie - "Very well."

[Willie signals The Specialist. He puts together the payment package.]

Gem - "Well, it's been fun. I'll see you bright and early Monday morning."

Willie - "I can tell that you are eager to get back to your family. But now that we've paid for it, would you mind showing us a quick demonstration?"

Gem - "You know, I don't actually start till Monday but, I'll make an exception. What would you like me to do?"

Willie - "Whatever you desire."

Gem Thinks - "He should have been more specific."

[Gem calmly stretches his hand a few feet and picks-up the bottle of Louis XIII. He places it on the bar in front of him.]

Willie - "Amazing!"

[Willie and The Specialist are standing in awe. Gem smiles at them / quickly raises his hand / shapes it into a mallet / SMASH! / Gem smashes the bottle of Louis and through the entire bar below it. Willie looks at the damage, looks at The Specialist, then looks at Gem and smiles.]

Willie - "That is precisely what I was looking for."

[They walk Gem out. The Specialist loads Gem's car.]

Willie - "I think that you and I will do great things together, Mr. Gem."

Gem Thinks - "I think he's right. I'm just not sure if our definitions of 'great' are the same."

Gem - "I guess we'll find out soon."

[They shake hands and part ways. Gem to hide his stash and then go back to the hospital. Willie, to do God knows what.]

CHAPTER FIVE:

LET THE GAMES BEGIN

[Day 1]

[Monday, 7:45AM. Gem arrives at Willie's Mansion, for the first day of the research / training.]

Gem Thinks - "Wow! This place looks even bigger in the daylight. Look at it! Whose salad did this guy have to toss to get this joint?"

[Gem rings the doorbell / guard opens the door.]

Guard - "Good morning, Mr. Gem. You are a bit early, let me see if Mr. Dietrich is available."

[The guard walks away. Gem starts looking around and sees a really interesting looking sculpture. He picks it up to look at it / drops it / it brakes. He looks around to see if anyone saw him / puts it back like nothing happened. Willie comes out to greet Gem.]

Willie - "Ahh...Mr. Gem. Please excuse the delay. We've been hard at work preparing our staff and facilities for you."

[Willie ushers Gem through a hallway towards the back of the house, to a set of large French-doors, overlooking the yard. Gem gazes at the site.]

It's a full-blown obstacle course, like the ones you see on those TV shows. Except, everything here is at least twice as big and ten-times as scary. Pegs, ropes, chains, walls, tubes; shit to chop, cut, stab, smash, climb over, go under... impale; you get the drift.

Willie - "This is where we will be testing and helping to develop, your physical abilities. Spectacular, isn't it? This is why I wanted you to see it in the daylight so, you could appreciate its splendor. And that's not all. Right over there, we're building a 4-story glass building for you to train on as well. Let's go downstairs. I want to introduce you to a couple of people."

That 'building' looks pretty, fuckin' flimsy, to me. It's just a plywood-reinforced scaffolding, covered with glass. I think I'd like to knock that thing over before we're done here. You know, just for shits-and-giggles.

[They make their way outside and down a brick staircase to the yard.]

Willie - "Ah, here comes your trainer now. Mr. Gem, I would like you to meet Mr. Steve Kutner."

[Gem and Steve shake hands and exchange greetings.]

Willie - "Mr. Kutner comes to us by way of the Navy Seals. First as an operative and then as a trainer. He is excellent in developing physical potential as well as mental awareness."

Gem - "I look forward to your tutelage, Mr. Kutner."

Mr. Kutner - "My friends call me Kutty."

Gem - "Kutty. What a cool name."

Kutty - "After what I've heard; I can't wait to start."

Willie - "Right this way, Mr. Gem. There is one more person I would like for you to meet."

[Willie leads Gem back into the house, through the entrance to the walkout basement. They walk into the lab. A woman comes in right behind them. She's holding a clipboard in her left hand and a fresh cup of coffee in her right. She puts on a big, fake smile, the minute she sees Gem.]

Willie - "Mr. Gem, allow me to introduce you to Miss Svetlana Morgan. She comes to us by way of several top research clinics. She is considered invaluable in her ability to decipher complex cases, such as yours."

Miss Morgan - "Just Lana, please."

Interesting; Russian first name, English last name and a bit of an accent. Gotta watch what I say in Russian around her.

Gem - "Just Gem."

[Gem goes to shake Lana's hand, and accidentally knocks her coffee on her.]

Gem - "Sorry about that."

[Lana, standing there, dripping but, still smiling.]

Gem Thinks - "What the fuck is with that plastic smile? She didn't even lose it when I spilled hot coffee on her. Who does that?"

Lana - "I'm going to go clean-up. I'll be right back."

[Lana making her way out of the room. Still has that fake plastic smile on her face. Gem watches her walk out, fake smiling back at her.]

Willie - "There is one other person, that you will be working with directly."

[Gem looks down the hall and sees an imposing looking figure coming towards them.]

Gem - "Let me guess, this one's coming to us by way of the S.S.?"

Willie - "He will be the one coordinating between the training and the research study. He will be responsible for collecting all the information and compiling it for us. If there's anything you need, you can go to him."

[The imposing figure gets closer and steps into the light. Gem sees that it's The Specialist.]

Gem - "Oh, it's just you. The way Willie was carrying-on, I thought it was going to be someone important."

The Specialist - "Mr. Gem, I assure you that I am quite capable in my duties. Please feel free to let me know, if there's anything I can do to be of help."

Gem Thinks - "Oh, this could be fun. I've never had a personal errand-boy before."

Gem - "I certainly will."

[Willie escorts Gem back outside, where Lana and Kutty are waiting for him.]

Willie - "Well then, now that we're all acquainted, I am going to leave you in Lana and Steve's, very capable hands. Please let us know if there is anything at all that you may need."

[Willie walks away. Gem looks around the premises.]

This guy's got guards all over the place. There's one assigned to Lana, there's one assigned to Steve and others scattered all over the property. Now, I understand why a douche-bag like Willie would need protection. But, why Lana and Steve? Do they think they need protecting from me? Or are the guards there to make sure that they don't stray?

[It starts.]

Lana - "Okay, Mr. Gem..."

Gem - "Just to let you know, I'm not calling anyone here mister or miss anything. So please, pretty please, with sugar on top, just Gem."

Lana - "Okay...Gem, before we start on anything else today, I would like to check your vitals and get samples from you, as well."

Gem - "Okay."

[Lana opens a case with a bunch of medical crap in it.]

Lana - "I'm going to check your blood pressure, heart rate and oxygen levels. Then, I'm going to need to get a blood sample, urine sample and a saliva swab. These are all for our baseline. I will be performing this examination routine every morning."

Gem - "That's all fine, as long as you don't MRI me."

Kutty - "Yeah, I heard about that. Shot you right through a wall?"

Lana - "It did what?"

Gem - "Well, since my body now has shit-load of silver in it, the strong magnetic field, shot me out like a missile."

[Kutty starts laughing hard / Lana puts on a big, fake grin.]

Gem Thinks - "There's that freaky shit again. What is with this chick?"

Kutty - "Now, how about we see what you can do on the course?"

[Kutty walks Gem around the entire obstacle course and explains what needs to be done in each segment.]

Kutty - "Just do what you're comfortable with. This is just a starting point. Are you ready?"

Gem - "Ready"

Kutty - "Go!"

I start on the course. I'm basically just using my regular abilities, with just a little bit of the silver stretching mixed in. I'm going slow because, I don't want to show too much, just yet. I just want to give them a few little pieces to build on. I see Kutty and Lana looking at each other. It looks like they're surprised by my lack of abilities. Look at them, each time I screw-up, I see they're shaking their heads in disbelief. Willie must have shown them that video he has of me.

[Gen finishes the course in terrible fashion / barely using any powers.]

Gem - "So, how'd I do?"

Kutty - "If my dead grandma was out there, she would have smoked your ass! That was pathetic, even for someone who's overweight, has asthma and no special powers at all."

Gem - "Yeah...sorry about that. I still don't have full control of this new skill."

Kutty - "Well then, let's see what you can control."

So, I pretend to strain and concentrate. I turn my arms silver and begin to stretch. I turn my hands silver and start forming them into mallets. Then, swoop, I bring it all back to normal.

Kutty - "That was amazing! Where was that on the course?"

Gem - "I tried but, it requires a lot of concentrating. It's hard to do it quickly and in a fluid motion."

Kutty - "Then that's what we'll be working on first. Once we get that down, you will have the capacity and confidence to build on it."

[Lana is standing there with that plastic smile still on her face. She seems disappointed.]

Lana - "Yes...that was...great. I'm just going to go check the test results and be right back."

[Lana walks back towards the lab. Gem waits for her to get out of hearing range and turns to Kutty.]

Gem - "What is her problem?"

Kutty - "I don't know. She seemed so interested in working with you. After Mr. Dietrich showed us the video yesterday, all she did was plan for your arrival. She was excited, almost gitty. And now...not so much."

Whatever. I'm just going to stay outside with Kutty for most of the day. I like him, he seems like a straight shooter.

[Gem and Kutty start working on stretching in morphing techniques. Gem shows more and more throughout the day but, still holding back a lot. Lana stays in the lab running tests for the rest of the day. She watches them occasionally, through the window. It's end of day.]

Kutty - "You did a good job out there today. After how you started, I was quite nervous. But after seeing how much you've improved, in just one day, I'm proud of you."

Believe it or not, that actually felt good. I can't remember the last time that somebody I respected; told me they were proud of me.

[Gem thanks Kutty and shakes his hand. As he's passing by the lab window, he waves to Lana. She waves back but, flashes that fake smile again.]

Gem Thinks - "What a fucking nut-job."

[Gem leaves for the day / drives back to the hospital to check on his kids / tells Natasha about what's going on and about the people he's working with. Kutty...cool. Lana...nice but, fake and creepy. He goes home to clean up / he's thinking about everything / goes back to the hospital and sleeps by his kids.]

****

[Day 2]

[Tuesday, 7:45AM. Gem arrives at the Mansion for the second day of the research sessions. He goes straight to the yard and greets Kutty.]

Gem - "What's up, Kutty?"

Kutty - "How you doin', Gem?"

Gem - "Where's Smiley?"

Kutty - "I think she's in the lab."

[Gem looks over at the lab / sees Lana speaking with The Specialist. He looks stone-faced as usual.]

Gem - "What a ray of sunshine that guy is. What's he doing?"

Kutty - "He's getting the information from yesterday. He was here earlier getting my reports, too."

Gem - "Should we wait?"

Kutty - "I don't know how long she's going to be. Let's get started and she can run her tests when she's done. I think we should work on the things we know you can do, just to give you more control over them. Then, we can expand from there."

Gem - "Sounds good. What should we work on first?"

Kutty - "Let's work on a stretching part first."

Gem - "Okay."

[Kutty places a can several feet away from Gem.]

Kutty - "Alright now, I want you to imagine that in that can, are the answers to all of your questions. And all you have to do, is reach out and get it."

Gem - "Okay."

[Gem pretends to try to stretch / straining / little happening / arms go out a few extra feet.]

Gem - "Sorry. It's like it has a mind of its own."

Kutty - "Gem, let me explain what I'm trying to do here. Yesterday, you told me that it requires a lot of concentration for your abilities to present themselves. My goal, is to get you to do it so often, that it becomes second nature to you. I know it's hard but, with practice, it will get easier."

[Lana walks up to them. Fake smile on, again.]

Lana - "Mr. Gem..."

Gem - "Jesus! Just Gem, please."

Lana - "I have to perform the daily exam."

Gem - "Okay...where's your little case of goodies?"

Lana - "Mr. Sauer said that all testing is to be conducted in the lab, to lessen the chance of contamination. Shall we?"

[They all walk into the lab. Lana runs all the same tests from yesterday. Gem starts to walk out.]

Lana - "We're not quite finished yet. Since you can't be MRI'd, I would like to do a full body x-ray. And, I will also need a sperm sample; I forgot to get that yesterday."

Gem Thinks - "Sperm sample...I wonder if she's gonna perform that herself, too?"

Gem - "Okay."

[Gem undresses and puts on an exam gown. Lana begins to run the 360-degree, X-Ray Scan.]

What the fuck was that?! I just felt a burst of energy hit me as soon as she flipped-on that x-ray switch. It's tingling, warm, stating to tickle a bit.

Gem - "Ummm, something feels weird here."

[The scan finishes / Lana and Kutty walk back into the room and stare at Gem, with their mouths wide open. Gem is glowing. When he moves, it's as if his molecules are separating, they're lagging and can't keep up with his movements. Gem looks at his hands in bewilderment.]

Gem - "Is this good or bad?"

[Lana and Kutty are still staring at Gem, they don't know what to do.]

Gem - "What the fuck people?! Do something! I'm falling apart here!"

[Lana and Kutty start to scramble around.]

Gem - "How do I get this energy out of me? I can feel it in every cell of my body!"

Lana - "Does it hurt?"

Gem - "No. It actually feels tingly, warm and somewhat serine. I'm just freaking out because, I'd rather stay intact!"

Lana - "You need to discharge."

Gem - "You mean jerk-off?"

Lana - "No, you idiot! Like when you discharge static electricity, by touching something metal.]

[Gem tries to touch a metal table but, his hand goes right through it.]

Gem - "What the...did you see that? I'm like a freaking ghost!"

Kutty - "Try to push it out. Concentrate your energy on your hands and try to push it out."

[Gem tries once, twice, third time...nothing. Just tiny pieces of him, flying-off, then gravitating back to him. Kutty runs out of the room. Gem and Lana are standing there, looking at each other. They're both nervous. Kutty comes running back, with a pepper shaker in hand. He opens it up and pours some pepper into the palm of his hand.]

Lana - "Pepper?"

Kutty - "Gem, close your eyes and breathe in through your nose. Let's see, if this will get him the discharge he needs."

[Kutty blows the pepper around Gem / he sneezes. First sneeze, his body expands and contracts.]

Kutty - "Try taking a deeper breath."

[Gem takes in a huge breath. Then, lets out a big, loud sneeze. His body rapidly expands, then quickly pops back in place, with a blast of energy. The blast blew-out some of the equipment in the room. Willie and The Specialist come running into the lab. Willie looks around in amazement.]

Willie - "Now, we're making progress. What caused this miraculous discovery?"

[Lana looks at Gem, Kutty and her guard, who was also in the lab when it happened.]

Lana - "I'm not sure. I think it was some sort of electrical discharge but, I'm not sure what caused it. We will investigate everything and have a full report by end of day."

[Gem, Kutty and the guard, all look at Lana curiously.]

Gem Thinks - "I wonder why she's holding back?"

Willie - "Please, make sure not to leave out any details. This is a very exciting development."

[Willie and the specialist walk away.]

Lana - "Did you know you could do that?"

Gem - "No. Why do you think I was freaking out?"

[Gem looks at Kutty.]

Gem - "Thank you."

Kutty - "No problem. I'm just glad it worked. I couldn't think of anything else."

[Lana hands Gem a large test-tube.]

Lana - "I think this may be a good time for that sperm sample."

Gem - "No, thank you. After what just happened, I'm not really in the mood."

Lana - "That's exactly why I would like to get the sample now, to see if after what just happened, it will be different from future samples."

[Gem looks at the test-tube.]

Gem - "Are you shittin' me?! You want me to jerk-off into this thing? I mean, even if my aim is perfect. You gotta remember, I've been out for months; zero ejaculations. I probably have enough baby-batter in me to fill a mayonnaise jar."

[Gem and Kutty look at each other and laugh. Lana gets her fake smile back on.]

Lana - "Mr. Gem..."

Gem - "Oh my God! Again with that Mr. Gem, shit."

Lana - "Sorry...Gem."

Gem - "Yes?"

Lana - "The average male ejaculates about 5 ml. That is a 30 ml test-tube. It is highly unlikely that you will have overflow. Also, at this time, it happens to be the only sterile receptacle that I have."

[She stares at him with her freaky, fake smile.]

Gem Thinks - "If I have to look at this face for another minute, overflow won't be my problem, no-flow will be."

Gem - "Fine."

[Gem picks-up a bottle of lotion from Lana's work area.]

Gem - "Ooooo...lavender."

Lana - "I'm afraid you can't use that. It will contaminate the sample."

Gem - "Really? You're gonna make me dry-jerk?"... "Fine!"... "Sadist."

[Gem grabs the test-tube and Lana's tablet computer and goes into the bathroom. Sounds begin to emanate from the bathroom. It's Japanese porn, with lots of moaning, talking and noise making, turned up to full volume. Lana and Kutty stare at the door, then start to fidget around to keep busy. Gem comes out a few minutes later.]

Gem - "Wow! That was quick, even for me. That video was awesome!"

[Gem looks at Kutty.]

Gem - "I'll send you the link."

Kutty - "Yes, please do."

[Gem turns to Lana.]

Gem - "Good news. We were both right. There was no overflow, just like you said. But I was right too, the opening was way too small. I told you, it's been a while. The shit went-off like a God-damn fire hose."

[Gem takes Lana's bare hand and sticks a dripping, wet test-tube into it. Splat! He stares at her with his sarcastic grin, she's looking back at him with her fake smile, as usual.]

Gem - "Isn't that great?"

[Gem places his wet (from the test-tube) hand on to Lana's shoulder. He pats her as-if he's congratulating her but, she knows what he's doing, as he cleans his hand on her lab coat.]

Gem - "I just love a win-win situation."

[He hands Lana her tablet.]

Gem - "Oh, and thanks for this. It was very helpful. Sorry, I got some stuff on it too. I think I wiped it all off but, you might wanna go over it again, just in case."

[Gem walks out of the lab. Kutty right behind him. Lana still standing there, with the dripping sample in one hand and the sticky tablet in the other. She finally lost that fake smile. She looks at her assigned guard, in a disappointed way. Gem and Kutty get back to the yard.]

Gem - "I love fucking with her. She's so uptight! And that freaky smile...what a dip-shit."

[Gem imitates Lana's fake smile.]

Gem - "I mean really, can you imagine living with that?"

[Lana is looking through the window. She knows that Gem is making-fun of her. She continues watching them as she runs her tests.]

Kutty - "You ready to give this another go?"

Gem - "Let's do it!"

[Gem gets ready, and goes. A little better again today. Better stretching, quicker moves but, he's still holding back. Gem finishes the course. Still hasn't chopped, smashed or stabbed anything.]

Kutty - "That was much better. Your time has improved and I see you're feeling a lot more comfortable out-there."

Gem - "I guess it's because of all the good advice you've been giving me."

Kutty - "That may be part of it but, I think it's mostly you, getting used to your abilities."

[Gem stays with Kutty through lunch and the entire second half of the day. As he's leaving, Gem waves to Lana. She quickly waves back; the plastic smile is plastered on her face, again. Gem goes back to the hospital and spends the night with his family, as usual.]

****

[Day 3]

[Wednesday, 7:48AM. Gem arrives at the mansion and makes his way to the yard.]

Gem - "Kutty."

Kutty - "Gem."

[As they're shaking hands, Lana walks up to them. She's fake-smiling but, not as much as usual. She looks tired, nervous.]

Lana - "Gem?"

Gem - "Oh my God! I'm so proud of you! You finally dropped the 'mister' shit."

Lana - "I have to do my exams."

Gem - "What's wrong, Lana? You don't seem quite as cheerful today."

Lana - "I'm sorry, I'm just really tired."

Gem - "Oh, I wasn't complaining. It's a nice change of pace from what we've been seeing."

Kutty - "You two go ahead. I'm going to stay here and make a few adjustments."

[Gem and Lana head into the lab. Lana begins her examinations.]

Lana - "Gem...may I speak candidly with you for a moment?"

Gem - "Sure. What's up, Smiley?"

Lana - "Gem, I think that you and I got off on the wrong foot."

Gem - "Awww...why do you say that?"

[Lana still sporting her plastic grin. But, it's fading fast.]

Lana - "I took this opportunity for a very specific purpose."

Gem Thinks - "I bet ya did."

Gem - "Yeah? And what's that? To study me like a fucking lab rat, so you can win some fucking science award? I saw how excited you were when I was freaking out. Probably thinking that I was going to fall apart and die. That would make for an interesting research paper."

Lana - "I wasn't excited. I was scared too."

Gem - "Scared for me or about your stupid project? I don't remember you saying 'are you okay Gem?' or 'please sit down and take a rest, Gem'. No, what I remember is you sending me to dry-jerk, right after the incident."

[Lana looks at Gem. She doesn't know what to say. She flashes the smile again.]

Gem - "Oh, and there's that freaky, fuckin' smile again! What is wrong with you? Everything about you seems too fake and too planned. I don't like you. You're fake and you have your own agenda."

Lana - "I'm not fake!"

Gem - "Bullshit! You've been fake since the second I met you. The only time you spoke with me honestly, is when you called me an 'idiot' yesterday. Why can't you just...speak from the heart. I'd rather you be a bitch to me, then fake."

[Lana loses her smile.]

Gem Thinks - "Oh, shit! What's about to happen here?"

Lana - "Okay, Gem. You want me to speak from my heart and tell you what I truly think?"

Gem Thinks - "Fuck! Now I'm not so sure I do. Why did I even bring it up?"

Lana - "I think that you don't deserve this gift. I think that any normal person would have applied himself from the very beginning, to try to develop this power and use it for something great and beneficial to society. And, I think that you are an irresponsible, asshole, who's bad judgment nearly killed him as well as his entire family. The fact that you exist at all, makes me question everything I know about science and my faith."

[This was more than Gem bargained for. He's hurt. He knows she's right, at least about the "irresponsible asshole" part.]

Gem - "Okay...see, that wasn't so hard. We're finally making some progress. Now, if you'll excuse me, I have something in my eye."

[Gem walks away, looking like he's about to cry. He goes back to the yard and wipes his eyes.]

Kutty - "You alright?"

Gem - "What a bitch! I fucking hate her! First, she starts-off all fake and lovey-dovey; and now, crazy, psycho, bitch!"

Kutty - "First off, let me just say this; I know what you're saying. I see the plastic smile and fake cheeriness too. But she wasn't like this before you got here. The time we spent together, before you got here, she was nothing but professional. She would look you in the eye, make her point clearly, listen attentively, make and take criticism well...very, very businesslike. She barely showed any emotion the whole time. I don't think I saw her smile once. She was very interested in you. Couldn't wait to meet you. Then you get here, she throws-on that clown-face and she's an entirely different person."

Gem - "I know! She just told me she took this job for a specific reason."

Kutty - "Did she say what that reason was?"

Gem - "No! She just started saying how I didn't deserve this and some other really mean shit."

Kutty - "Well, maybe she had a very different perception of who you were, before you got here?"

Gem - "So, it's not my fault if she's disappointed. It's her fault for expecting too much from someone she didn't even know."

Kutty - "You're right. But aren't you at all curious, as to what her reason was for taking the job?"

Gem - "My guess is, to test me to my limits, kill me, dissect me, get paid for doing it and maybe even win some sort of prize for it."

Kutty - "Maybe? But don't you want to find out, before she goes?"

[Kutty nods in the direction of the lab. Gem looks over and sees that Lana is gathering her belongings.]

Gem - "God damn it."

[Gem walks back into the lab. Lana looks up at him, with tears in her eyes, as she continues packing her things.]

Gem - "You just tore me a new one and now you're the one crying? What are you, bipolar?"

Lana - "I'm not bipolar."

Gem - "So, just the fake, depressed, bitchy side then, huh?"

[Lana tries to ignore Gem and hold back her tears, as she continues to pack.]

Gem - "What's your reason?"

[Lana still trying to ignore him.]

Gem - "What is your 'very specific purpose' for taking this job?"

[Lana looks at Gem. Her tears roll down her face.]

Lana - "It doesn't matter anymore. I now see that you lack the capacity, both physical and mental."

Gem - "You sound disappointed in me."

Lana - "That's an understatement. There are a million people out there, better suited than you, to have these abilities. Not to mention, a lot more responsible than you."

Gem - "Well, there you have it."

Lana - "What?"

Gem - "You solved your own dilemma."

[Lana looks a Gem, confused.]

Gem - "That's why those million people don't have these powers...they're too fucking responsible."

Lana - "What?!"

Gem - "Don't you see the irony here? It's my lack of responsibility that gave me these abilities."

Lana - "I so don't like you."

Gem - "It's okay, I understand. I'm not for everyone. Only for those with very discriminating palates. I'm like an acquired taste. You know, like a beer, wine, Shakespeare... Rocky Mountain Oysters. Things that most people don't really like at first but, many are intrigued enough to come back for more. And before you know it, I'm an old favorite."

Lana - "Did you just compare yourself to a dish made from a bull's testicles?"

Gem - "Is that what those things were? What the fuck?"

[Gem smiles at Lana and she gives a little smile back.]

Gem - "See, now there's an authentic smile. Now come-on, tell me why you're really here."

[Lana hesitates and looks at her assigned guard. The guard looks at her and reluctantly nods his head, just a tiny bit. Gem notices the exchange but, doesn't say anything.]

Lana - "I'm here because of my son. He's a sweet, 9-year-old boy with a medical condition. He has what's called a Brain Stem Glioma. It's an inoperable tumor in his brain which, is slowly growing and is starting to impede his brain function. If left untreated, it will kill him. Now imagine my excitement, when I heard of a man who can bend and stretch his fingers at will. I thought maybe, just maybe there might be a way for you to help me, help my son. I was hoping that you might be able to bend and form your fingers into extensions, in such a way, as to go around the sensitive tissue and remove the mass."

Really? It couldn't have been a more perfect scenario for a guilt-trip. Now, I'm not one to walk away from a child in need but, this is some really serious shit. But if I help him, maybe it'll score me some extra karma points. And I could really use that right now.

Gem - "I'm willing to help, in any way I can."

Lana - "Thank you, Gem. But I don't see how you can. No offense but, with your learning curve, it would take a hundred years to get you ready."

Gem - "I think you'll find, that with me, when there's a will, I'll always find a way. But you'll owe me big-time."

Lana - "If by some miracle, you can do this; anything you want."

Gem - "I like the way you think."

[Gem gets a piece of paper and writes something on it. Puts it into an envelope and seals it. He hands it to Lana.]

Gem - "What I want, is written inside that envelope. Don't open it until after I'm done with my part of the deal. Got it?"

Lana - "Wait. What's it say?"

Gem - "What's the difference? You said anything I want."

[Lana nods her head in agreement. Gem smiles at her, stands-up and calls Kutty.]

Gem - "Hey, Kutty! Come quick! I just did something really cool!"

[Gem turns to Lana and smiles.]

Gem - "Did you really think I haven't been practicing this shit, with every spare second I have?"

[Kutty comes running in to the lab.]

Kutty - "What'd you do?"

[Gem holds out his hand and starts extending his fingers out.]

Gem - "Watch this. I can extend my fingers, while at the same time, make them bend at certain points."

Kutty - "Would you look at that. The bends are staying at the same points, while the fingers are still extending outward. Amazing! How are you doing that?"

Gem - "I don't know."

[Gem looks over at Lana. She's real-smiling, ear-to-ear. Eyes, wide as dinner plates. She just got her hope back.]

Gem - "I guess, I just stopped trying to do it with my brain and tried doing it with my heart."

Kutty - "Not thinking, seems to really be working for you."

Gem - "Yeah, I should've stopped using my brain a long time ago."

[Gem and Kutty chuckle. They look over at Lana, she's already hard at work. She looks excited, happy. They leave her to her work and go back out to the obstacle course.]

Gem - "You knew what her reason was?"

Kutty - "Yes."

Gem - "You knew that I would be willing to help her?"

Kutty - "Yes."

Gem - "How did you know that I could?"

Kutty - "That, I wasn't so sure about. But I do know that you're holding back. I knew it from the first day. I told you, Mr. Dietrich showed us the video he has of you; healing after getting shot and morphing your hand through a grate. He also showed us the damage you did in his bar."

[Gem looks away.]

Kutty - "Predicting the outcome with Lana, was easy. You both have children in bad predicaments. That commonality and your love of children, made that a safe bet. My question to you is, why are you holding back so much?"

Gem - "For the same reasons you just gave. I have nothing in common with that dip-shit, Willie or his ambitions. And my love for children, is why I don't want him to succeed. I don't think he's focusing on the 'medical breakthrough' aspect of this. I think he's focusing on the 'weaponization' side of things. There's much more money to be made on that front."

Kutty - "Are you worried that they're going to sell silver-soldiers off to the highest bidders?"

Gem - "Actually, I'm more worried they'll keep the soldiers for themselves. And if they do, who would stop them from taking over? These are not the kind of people that want to destroy everything. They are the kind that create chaos, fear and instability. That way, they take things over intact."

Kutty - "What are you getting at, Gem?"

[Gem gets closer to Kutty.]

Gem - "What I've shown you, is just some of what I know I can do. And I'm sure there's more that I don't even know about. And I'm also sure, that shit, is gonna be even crazier than the shit I already know about."

[Kutty looks concerned.]

Kutty - "We have a job to do here, an assignment that we both signed up for. And I don't know about you but, when I make a deal, I intend to keep my side of the bargain."

Lana - "He's not asking you to break your deal."

[Gem and Kutty are both surprised to hear Lana. She's been standing behind them long enough to hear Gem's concerns.]

Lana - "He's just asking you to 'redact' some of the information. You were in the Navy Seals, I'm sure you've seen your share of creatively edited reports."

Kutty - "That I have."

Gem - "Can you imagine yourself or those young men you train, facing a bunch of me in combat? A bunch of assholes, butchering them at will."

Lana - "I'm still having trouble dealing with one asshole like you."

Gem - "Ha, ha. Very funny. I think I liked you better when you weren't being you."

Kutty - "Why don't we call it a day? I've got a lot to think over."

Gem - "Okay, I wanted to go home before the hospital anyway."

Lana - "I got a bunch of data to sort through, too"

Gem - "Just tell 'The Specialist' I was tired and went home."

[They part ways.]

****

[Day 4]

[Thursday, 7:45 AM. Gem arrives at the mansion. He goes straight to the yard, as usual.]

Gem - "Kutty."

Kutty - "Gem."

Gem - "Did you have a chance to think about our conversation yesterday?"

Kutty - "Let's walk the course."

[They begin to walk the course. Kutty starts to talk, as soon as they're out of hearing distance for his guard.]

Kutty - "I was having a lot of trouble making my decision. You really put me in a tough spot. I don't like to break my word for anything. But as I was sitting there, contemplating what to do, I got a call from a friend of mine in the CIA. He said he was calling because he got a call from an old associate of his; an ex-KGB agent named Victor Petrov. Apparently, Victor was calling my friend to get information on Mr. Dietrich. I agreed to speak with Victor and answer any of his questions. It wasn't two minutes into the conversation, that we realized we had something in common...you. When I asked him about you, do you know what he said?"

Gem Thinks - "Shit! Please don't be the 'how we become friends' story."

Gem - "What did he say?"

Kutty - "He told me the story of how you two met."

Gem Thinks - "Oh, fuck!"

Gem - "Yeah, that's a funny story."

Kutty - "He said you beat him and almost killed him."

Gem - "He always exaggerates that story."

Kutty - "He mentioned power tools, chainsaw, knives, blowtorch, gasoline and a whole slew of other weapons. He said he was so scared he pissed himself."

Gem - "What a drama-queen."

Gem Thinks - "Fucking Victor."

Kutty - "I'm in."

Gem - "What? After all that?"

Kutty - "Well, he also said that you were the best friend he's ever had. That he owed his life to you. That he would kill or die for you. And for those KGB guys, the killing part is no big deal. The dying for someone part, that's not a common practice."

[The Specialist comes-up to them.]

The Specialist - "Mr. Dietrich would like to meet with everyone, in the lab."

[Gem and Kutty look at each-other, then follow The Specialist to the lab. Willie and Lana are already there.]

Willie - "I am becoming increasingly concerned, with the lack of progress that I've been seeing. Especially, out on the course. Mr. Kutner, do

I have to remind you of the terms of your contract. At this rate, I don't see how he'll be ready for the show."

Gem - "What show?"

[Everyone looks at each-other, surprised. They all knew about the show but, no-one told Gem.]

Willie - "Apparently, we all forgot to mention it. It's more of a presentation of your potential to some of our business associates. It's not a big deal. Just run through the obstacle course and the glass building, hit a few things along the way maybe, break something in the end."

Gem - "What the fuck?! I don't remember approving that! Need I remind you of the terms of our contract?!"

Willie - "I assumed..."

Gem - "You assumed incorrectly, Wilhelm! This is the kind of sneaky-shit that breaks trust. And I don't like it. Give me one good reason not to walk right now. And it better be very, fucking good."

Willie - "One 'Delivery' gold bar."

Gem - "No."

Willie - "Two."

Gem - "Done!"

I just funded my boys' education, and then some. In case you don't know, those things are 400 ounces, each. Do the math.

Gem - "Don't forget, everything in the contract, still applies; I decide."

Willie - "Of course."

Gem - "And I would like to have an off-site, team-building meeting, just for the rest of the morning. We've been working on parts, till now and I want to make sure we're all on the same page before we start putting everything together."

Willie - "I will call the country club. They will provide you with a private area and whatever else you may need."

Gem - "Thanks, Willie. I think it will be of great help."

Willie - "I certainly hope so."

[Gem, Lana and Kutty head out to the country club. When they arrive, they are provided a private area on the back terrace of the dining hall.]

Gem - "I called this meeting, to make sure we're all on the same team. Team 'Fuck-Willie', give him as little information as possible. Now,

Lana, I haven't got a direct confirmation from you yet but, from the way you've been acting, I assume you're in."

Lana - "I know who these people are. I've been in, since the beginning. Screw them all."

Gem - "That's the spirit. Now, I want us all to lay our concerns on the table. We need to do this so; it works out well for all of us."

Lana - "Well, I'm broke, my husband is out on assignment and my son is clinging on to his life, as we speak."

Gem - "How are you broke? You're a fuckin' doctor?!"

Lana - "We've spent everything; retirement plans, savings, even the money we had set aside for his college education. Experimental procedures are not covered by insurance and aren't cheap."

Gem - "Okay. Kutty?"

Kutty - "I don't get paid a dime unless you ace the show."

Gem - "What kind of shitty deal is that?"

Kutty - "He offered me a hundred-thousand dollars, if I did it that way. "

Gem - "You made that deal without even knowing me?"

Kutty - "I was willing to roll the dice because, I need the money for my retirement house. My amazing wife, spent the last thirty-plus years doing everything in her power, to make my life better. She really loves that house. It's big, on a lake with lots of fish, secluded. It would be the perfect house for us to be a family in. Plenty of room for the grandkids to stay and play. I get a decent pension and I do have some savings but, I needed that hundred-grand, to make it work. It's too bad. But, once again, duty calls."

Gem - "My main concern, is my boys. I would love it, if we found a way to help them. My second concern is, Slick-Willie finding out about the shit he doesn't know about."

Lana - "What are you hiding?"

Gem - "What I'm about to tell you, stays between us. I can hold and redirect electricity. I think that, once developed, it's going to be my strongest power. That is something he doesn't know about, and will not know about. Because that, opens too many new doors. Crazier doors. Agreed?"

Kutty - "Yes."

Lana - "Yes."

Gem - "Good. 'Cause God forbid, these powers fall into the wrong hands."

Lana - "They already have."

Gem - "You know, I'm starting to miss your clown-face."

Lana - "Sorry."

[Lana and Kutty smile at each-other.]

Gem - "Now, let me tell you a little something about playing for Team-Gem..."

Kutty - "I thought we were playing for 'Team Fuck-Willie'?"

Gem - "As I was saying, I take care of my teammates. I promise both of you, I will do everything in my power to fix your problems, too. I say, we go back and start showing some progress. He's already in nervous mode, I don't want to get him into desperation mode. Guys like that do bad things when they're desperate. And guys like us, get fucked in the process."

[They all agree, eat some lunch and head back to the mansion. Lana runs her daily exams. Afterwards, she stays in the lab to run her tests and get things ready for the surgery training. Gem and Kutty head out to the course.]

Gem - "Walk me through this again. Tell me what you need on each part."

As he's walking me through the course and explaining the "routine" again, this time, I'm actually paying attention. I like this guy and I'm not gonna let him leave here empty-handed."

Gem - "Kutty, I can do this. I can do every obstacle here, no problem. What I need to learn, is how to do it smoothly, gracefully."

Kutty - "Lucky for us, I train parkour."

Gem - "What's that?"

Kutty - "That's what's gonna get me paid."

[Kutty and Gem, spend the rest of the afternoon practicing parkour moves. Jumps, landings, rolls, leaping through stuff. He got more and more "graceful", as the day went on. Lana stops him, on his way out.]

Lana - "I have everything ready for tomorrow."

[Gem looks over her shoulder and sees a table full of 3D printed models of Lana's son's head, prints of different scans, an endoscope and an ultrasound.]

Gem - "Yes, I see."

Lana - "I'm so excited. Because, today when I look at his face, I can smile. We have hope again."

[Lana hugs Gem. Gem leaves to do his usual routine. A couple of hours later, Gem arrives at the hospital. As he's walking in, he sees Lana pull-up to the valet.]

Gem - "What are you, stalking me?"

Lana - "You wish. My son's here."

Gem - "So are my boys. Why don't you come with me, so I can introduce you to my family?"

Lana - "Okay. But, just for a minute."

Gem - "Don't worry, I wouldn't want it to be more than that, anyway. I get enough of you at work."

[They go to the boys' hospital room. Lana and Natasha hit-it-off, right from the start.]

Look at them, like a couple of yentas. I hear them making fun of me; my sarcasm, the "annoying gotch-ya grin" I usually display, my "exaggerated" hand gestures. Usually, I'd be teasing right back but, not today. Because today, I hear Natasha laughing; I see her having fun for the first time in, God knows how long? There is no-way in hell, that I'm gonna open my mouth and risk fucking this up for her. I'm just gonna sit here and let them have-at-it. I think Lana needs this too.

[Natasha and Lana tease Gem for a little while. Then, they both get-up to go visit Lana's son.]

Gem - "Can I come too?"

Lana - "It's never a good idea, for a surgeon to operate on someone he knows. You already have too much of a connection because, of our relationship. Let's not make it any worse."

Gem Thinks - "She called me 'surgeon'. Now it's getting serious. Great! Now I'm getting nervous."

[When Natasha returns, Gem tells her about his day. Then, she goes home to rest, while Gem stays with the boys.]

[Day 5]

[Friday, 7:20 AM. Gem arrives at the mansion. Lana and Kutty are not in yet. Gem heads to the yard and starts practicing the parkour moves from yesterday. Willie comes out onto the terrace.]

Willie - "You seem to have a renewed vigor, this morning."

Gem - " I think the meeting yesterday really helped us get things strait."

[Willie comes down from the terrace and walks closer to Gem.]

Willie - "I believe I owe you an apology. It was wrong of me to surprise you with new expectations. I sincerely hope, that I didn't do any irreversible damage to our relationship."

Gem - "I forgive you Willie. Besides, you made up for it. But, I think we'd both be better-off, if we communicate more openly with each-other."

Willie - "I couldn't agree more."

Gem - "So, tell me what's going on so, I know how to make it work for everyone."

Willie - "Very well. A week from this Tuesday, I have dozens of business associates coming to see my 'find'. Some of these people are current clients of our organization and some are potential clients. They are all very powerful and well-connected. My goal is to impress them. To get them to do more business with us, as well as new business from the prospects."

Gem - "What's the glass building for? Is that going to be part of the show too?"

Willie - "Yes, a very important part. It will be the 'theatrical' part of the production."

Gem - "How do you have it planned?"

Willie - "We were thinking of having different scenarios set-up on each level. A helicopter brings you in, you come in through the top and handle each crisis as you work your way down. When you reach the ground level, there will be a couple of mock guards for you to 'handle', in some way."

Gem - "Sounds a little like the video for the song 'Hero' by the Foo-Fighters. Hey, we should use that song for the show. It will be perfect."

Willie - "I believe Mr. Sauer is putting that part together himself."

Gem - "Let me guess, he's gonna have some Euro-techno bullshit playing, isn't he? Tell him he can have the choreography but, I'm insisting on that song."

Willie - "I will let him know."

Gem - "Willie, when this show's done, you're going to want to give me a bonus."

Willie - "That's highly unlikely, considering you've already cost me much more than I planned."

Gem - "You'll see."

[Kutty walks up to Gem and Willie.]

Kutty - "Good morning, gentlemen."

Willie - "Good morning, Mr. Kutner. I'll be going, to leave you two to your work."

Kutty - "Everything okay?"

Gem - "Yes. Because, now I know what needs to be done, for everyone."

Kutty - "I saw Lana on the way in. She was almost running, like she was gitty, or something. Real smile, and everything."

Gem - "Good. That's just how I like my teammates. And don't worry Kutty, we'll take care of you too."

Kutty - "You know what's funny Gem? I don't have the slightest doubt, that you're sincere about that."

Gem - "Good. Now, let me go do my stuff with Lana and I'll be back to show you all the cool stuff I've been practicing."

[Gem walks into the lab to find Lana standing there, gitty.]

Lana - "Good morning, Gem."

Gem - "Hello, Lana."

[Gem looks around the lab. Even more stuff for the surgery training.]

Lana - "I got everything we need. When do you want to start?"

Gem - "Let's do it this afternoon. I've got a couple of worried people to settle down first."

Lana - "No problem."

[They take care of the exams and Gem goes back to the yard.]

Kutty - "You ready?"

Gem - "Just one minute, I have an idea."

[Gem calls Willie, The Specialist and Lana, outside. He turns to Willie and The Specialist.]

Gem - "I know that things seem to be moving slower than you anticipated. Yesterday, my team and I, put together all the pieces we've been working on. I wanted you to see the progress, to help set your minds at ease."

[Gem gets set and begins to run through the course. He completes everything, smoothly, effortlessly.]

Gem - "What'd you think?"

[They're all in shock. Smiling ear-to-ear.]

Gem - "You could add some height and length to the obstacles, if you'd like. Put some more things for me to smash through, while you're at it. 'Cause, thanks to my team, this shit's too easy."

[They're still amazed and smiling.]

Gem Thinks - "Great! Now they're all gitty."

[Specialist turns and hugs Gem.]

The Specialist - "I am sorry I doubted your dedication. You have made me very happy."

Gem - "That's great! I'm happy you're happy. Now, please...stop hugging me."

[The Specialist un-clinches Gem.]

Gem - "Willie, did you know that I volunteered to help Lana with her son's medical condition?"

Willie - "Yes. I allowed it, as long as it doesn't take away from the demonstration."

Gem - "Take away from it? You'd be crazy not to make it part of it! We can get one of those operating rooms with a balcony and they can be in the audience. Imagine the looks on their faces, as they witness two medical marvels, happening at once. You want accolades, Willie? They'll be lining-up to suck your dick, after that."

Willie - "Mr. Sauer, please consult with Ms. Morgan and make all the necessary arrangements. Thanks to Mr. Gem's eloquent, form of persuasion; from now on, we have a dual focus."

Now, Lana doesn't have to pay for anything. See how this works? You get 'em gitty, then you get what you want. It works well with kids, too.

[Gem, Kutty and The Specialist stay out to plan "enhancements" to the course. After lunch, they all go into the lab to help plan for the surgery. Gem insists that everything be done as a team. More questions, more ideas, more answers.]

By the end of the day, everyone was happy. The obstacle course run, was beyond expectation. Lana's meeting went well too. We were all coming up with ideas, even Sauer-boy. Not only did he come-up with the idea of using a 4D ultrasound, he even said he'd have one here by Monday.]

Gem - "Wow! I'm impressed. No wonder they call you 'The Specialist'."

You should have seen how happy he was, when I said that. I don't think he got much positive feedback as a kid.

[They adjourn for the day. Everyone goes home for the weekend, happy.]

[First Weekend]

The weekend was a nice break from all the hoopla. Natasha and I, got a chance to really take-in everything that's been happening and get our bearings. Unfortunately, there is still no news on the kids' situation. On Sunday, Victor and his family came by with food and gifts. My and Natasha's moms came by with even more food and gifts. It almost felt like everything was back to normal. I really miss how we used to be. Nothing seems right without my boys.

****

[Second Week of Training.]

Each day, started off like before. Morning exams, followed by course training and adjustments. The glass building was completed over the weekend and we were also working on the choreography for that. I won't bore you with the play-by-play for each day but, I will give you the highlights.

[Day 6: Monday.]

Staying true to his word, The Specialist got us a 4D ultrasound. This thing is unbelievable! The high-frequency sound waves, barely cause any problems for me; just a little tingle. And you can see everything in 3d and in real-time. I wish they had one of these when we were getting ultrasounds done, during our two pregnancies. We made a lot of progress in the surgery planning. It's amazing how fast things progress, when you add some enthusiasm into the mix. Willie even had my boys' medical files and samples brought in, for a second examination and comparison, by our team.

[Day 7: Tuesday.]

Lana gave me some potentially good news about the boys. Turns-out, they have a ton of silver particles suspended in their blood. Just like I did, when I first got to the hospital. She said the difference was, the silver in me has bonded molecularly but, the silver in them is still suspended. She didn't know what the catalyst could have been. Definitely, something to pursue. And definitely, something not to tell Willie about. She also got a couple cadavers for me to practice on. It was the sickest shit ever! And not in a good way. Sticking your bare hands through flesh, touching bone, the squishy brain...sick! I know I'm going-in silver but, I can still feel it as though I wasn't. I've been washing my hands and pouring on hand sanitizer, like crazy.

Kutty and I, worked on me bending my limbs around corners, as I stretch; to shoot, grab and stab targets. He got the idea from watching "Plastic Man" cartoons, as a kid. Maybe Victor gave him the "why reinvent the wheel" speech too.

[Day 8: Wednesday.]

During the morning exams, Lana and I, came to the conclusion that the shock from the defibrillator, must have been the catalyst for the molecular bonding of the silver particles. Now, I can't just go in and start zapping my boys just to see what happens. I need to test it somehow. But how? Who else was...Natasha! Her hands! Lana is going to come by the hospital tonight, to get blood and skin samples from Natasha's hands. I really hope she finds something.

On the course, Kutty and The Specialist are concerned about the helicopter being able to make it to the glass building, at the same time the second part of the song begins. Even Willie came out to "help".

The Specialist - "Maybe, we can have Gem skip the helicopter and catapult him there."

Gem - "Yeah, that doesn't sound dangerous at all. What if I end up hitting one of the rotors? Hey, here's an idea; I'm made out of a non-ferrous metal, I can be shot like a projectile, with just a little electromagnetic flux. I know, why don't you just stick me into a rail-gun and see how far I go?"

[Willie, Kutty and The Specialist all look at each other, they like the idea.]

Gem - "I was being sarcastic, you assholes. Don't even think about it!"

I think I know what to do. I can try to sling-shot myself but, I'm not exactly elastic. Which means I would have to stretch out and pull back, very quickly. I'm not sure if it will work but, if it does, it will be much more entertaining than watching me get on and off a helicopter.

I spend the entire second half of the day with Lana and Kutty, in the lab. We work on me turning my finger into a tube, once I reach the mass. Next, Kutty finds a way of amplifying and fine tuning the waves of the ultrasonic generator through my hand, turning the tube into a small ultrasound probe. And since it couldn't be biopsied, we need something that can be tuned accurately and to a wide range of frequencies. Lastly, I create a second opening in the tube, which connects to a suction device that sucks out the debris. It's called "Ultrasonic Aspiration" and it's a way of breaking up and removing tumors.

[Day 9: Thursday.]

The course is upgraded. Bigger obstacles, moving targets, they even added a bunch of spring-loaded shit, that's gonna be flying at me from all directions. Some I'll destroy, some I'll avoid getting hit by. I tell Kutty to add a couple of poles at the top of the warped wall, which is now over a hundred feet tall. What are the poles for, you may ask? They're for me to try and sling-shot myself to the glass building, on the other side of the course. I have plenty of elevation, just got to get the angle and speed right. We did a few dry runs on the rest of the course and the building. Those parts, we're good with.

Two interesting things with Lana today. First, during the morning exams, Lana hands me some capsules:

Lana - "Here, take these."

Gem - "What are they?"

Lana - "Carbon and graphene."

Gem - "What are they for?"

Lana - "If they absorb properly and then bond to or layer between the silver particles, we may be able to create an environment in you, that can store a lot more energy. Or, they could form into carbon and graphene nano-structures. There are too many variables in your body and they make it hard to predict the outcome."

Gem - "Are the nano-structures good or bad?"

Lana - "Well, it could make your silver stronger or, there's a tiny, little chance it could make your entire body, every cell, so stiff and rigid, that it will paralyze you and eventually lead to a slow and painful death."

Gem - "I think I'll pass."

Lana - "I think we should take the chance."

Gem - "We? What chance, are you taking?"

Lana - "Think of it. You would become an ultra-capacitor."

Gem - "Yeah or lots of pain and death!"

Lana - "You would literally, physically be the most powerful person on Earth."

I thought about it for all of a second.

Gem - "God damn it! Give me the fucking things. But, if I start dying, I'm taking you with me."

The second interesting thing; there is silver in Natasha's hands! Now, I could tell Natasha what's going on and see if she'll let me shock her, to see if the silver bonds. Or I can just do it, piss her off in the process and then we'll know if it worked, right then, as she'll probably smack me for it. I think I'll go with option two. It's a little more risky but, it will get us the answer quicker.

Later, at the hospital, I gave Natasha a nice zap to her hands. When she came to and I explained what happened, she got pissed as hell and took a couple swings at me. Unfortunately, no silver hands. Shit! I was so sure this would work. Maybe the stuff needs time to bond? Oh well, it was worth a shot. I'll try again in a couple of days.

[Day 10: Friday.]

First thing in the morning, Lana comes-up and smacks me on the arm. Then, she starts lecturing me for zapping Natasha. When did these two yentas have a chance to talk? She said that what I did was "stupid" and "irresponsible". Well, duh! How do you think we got here?

After she finishes pummeling me with her selective adjectives, she actually says something I'm interested in hearing.

Lana - "I think I figured-out what happened to you during the x-ray procedure. I want to test it now while Sauer is in his meeting with Dietrich. But I need you to trust me."

Gem - "Okay..."

Lana - "I'm going to have to x-ray you again."

Gem - "No fucking way!"

Lana - "It's the only way to know for sure."

Gem - "To know what for sure? If it's gonna kill me?"

Lana - "If I thought that it could kill you, I would wait till after David's surgery to try it."

Fuck! She got me there. How can I argue that logic?

Gem - "Fine. But do we have to do my whole body?"

Lana - "We can try it on any part you'd like."

Gem - "How about my left pinkie?"

Lana - "Just pick a part and place it in front of the x-ray."

She turns on the x-ray and my pinkie starts getting warm then, it starts to break-apart again.

Lana - "Now, slowly try going through the table."

Gem - "Okay, I went through it, just like last time."

Lana - "Hold on a second."

Lana takes a paper-clip and x-rays it for a couple of seconds.

Lana - "This time, don't go through it. Just a gentle touch."

As my finger gets close, I can see the paper-clip begin to break-up too. Then, as soon as I touch it, I can feel our particles mingling. I can feel myself control the motion, separate and integrate the particles, at will. But it's getting weaker. The effects of the x-ray are wearing off. Apparently, I don't need to discharge the energy, it just dissipates over time. And not much time, at that.

Lana - "It's called 'Automatic Molecular Slippage' and it means that not only do your molecules move, shift and form as needed but, they also cause other molecules that you come in contact with, to do the same. When charged with electromagnetic radiation, you can manipulate molecules. Your body can actually break the metal down to its smallest, complete pieces and then reintegrate and molecularly bind them to each other. It's like creating an alloy."

Gem - "Holy-shit! We can use this to remove the fuckin' tumor. The is awesome! And you made me waste all that time practicing, for nothing."

Lana - "We're not even close to that. First of all, we don't know what it will do to his body, not to mention his brain. Second, we don't know what will happen if you get over-exposed to the radiation. I feel much more comfortable staying with the original plan."

Gem - "It's your call."

Then, Kutty comes in and tells me that the poles have been installed, on top of the warped wall. As I get up there, I'm a little nervous. I know it won't kill me but, I am ten stories high and the only practice I got was last night, at the hospital. I tried pulling myself though the cafeteria doorway. And that ended with me pulling my head out of a vending machine that I shot into, by accident.

First try: Way under shot. Went out about thirty feet then, plopped to the ground. Those landing shoulder-rolls Kutty taught me don't help for shit, if you don't have any forward momentum. I keep forgetting about the extra hundred-plus pounds, that I'm carrying around in silver weight.

Second try: Much better. Got most of the two-hundred feet I need, to get to the roof of the building. Still plopped to the ground, though.

Third time's the charm: I fling myself out, as hard as I can. As I get close to the building though, I realize that I'm coming in way too fast. I grab on to the ledge of the roof to keep from rolling off of it.

At least now, I know I can get the distance. But how do I get more control? Guess I'll have to figure that out over the weekend.

[Second Weekend.]

Saturday, was like last Saturday, family day. Victor came by, as usual. Believe it or not, he's still coming by every day with anything we may need. Lana was with us for most of the day too. Poor girl is nervous as shit, about the upcoming surgery. Her and Natasha spent most of the day comforting each-other. Then, a nice little surprise; Kutty shows up with his wife. At first glance, it was obvious that he married-up, just like I did. Her name is Sarah and she quickly fit right in with the other two yentas. Kutty and Victor reminisced about their covert-opps days. Afterwards, they all went to visit Lana's son, David, for a while. And me? I wasn't allowed to go, again. I just sat there, starring at my boys. I know there's something we're missing. But what? Should I try to shock them? What's the worst that could happen? As I finally got the balls to do it, I hear Natasha's voice and quickly sit back down. Probably a good thing. As desperate as I feel right now, who knows how far I would've gone.

Sunday, I spent the morning at the hospital. Later, I met Victor at my house. He came to help me figure-out how to stick the landing on the glass building. I called him because he's been on a roll, as far as ideas go. Plus, I think he's been feeling a little left out lately. He was very excited to work on the powers again.

Victor - "I know, flying squirrels!"

Gem - "Really? Fucking squirrels? And here I thought you were getting useful."

Victor - "I see them before on Discovery Channel. They have extra skin between front and back legs, so they can glide through air to other tree. Then, before they land, they curve body, like letter 'c' and that slows them so, they don't crash."

Gem - "I like the not crashing part but, I want something a bit more theatrical."

Victor - "Then you need wings, like flying monkeys from Oz movie."

For a guy who supposedly has such a glamorous and adventurous life, this fucker sure does spend a lot of time in front of the tube.

Gem - "You know, the 'wings' part I liked. But was the flying monkeys analogy really necessary?"

Victor - "Sorry. I was looking at you then, I think of wings then, I picture flying monkeys."

Gem - "Thanks Vic. Next time, stop at 'sorry'. Your explanation didn't really help."

Victor - "And don't forget tail."

Gem - "What do I need a tail for? I'm just gliding."

Victor - "Tail changes angle of attack, controls direction of flight. And not monkey tail; bird or plane type tail."

Gem - "Congratulations! You're back to being useful."

We went to one of Victor's warehouses and practiced from the roof. And after several failed attempts, I think I finally got it.

[Day 11: Monday.]

It's the day before the show. Lana skipped the morning exams to make time for one more practice run, on a cadaver. I still can't get used to sticking my hands into a body. Kutty came up with a great idea; PTFE coating my body. What is PTFE? It's that non-stick coating they put on cookware, (who's brand name I can't use because it's trademarked). Why? 'Cause, not only will it make me slicker and not allow shit to stick to me but, it also provides unparalleled protection from all types of acids. And that's something that I've been looking for. Lana refused to let me get the coating, prior to the surgery. She's afraid to make any changes. I can't blame her. Kutty scheduled an appointment for the coating for Saturday, a day after our work here is done.

Once I finished the practice on the cadaver, I went out to the yard for final preparations. I practiced the gliding and landing part. It went well, I nailed the landing and everything after that. Willie and The Specialist were besides themselves with joy.

As the day ended, everyone was happy, smiling, patting each-other on the back. But it's not over yet. I still have to perform.

[Day 12: Tuesday. Day of the Show.]

Today is the day. I arrive to the mansion. This place is bustling with people getting the food, drinks, dining hall and the terrace, prepared for the guests. Willie and The Specialist are busy directing all the staff. I go into the lab to check on my team.

Lana is going through her checklist for the surgery tomorrow. I could tell she's nervous. She's afraid that something might go wrong, that I will somehow get hurt and not be able to perform the surgery tomorrow. Pretty shitty planning, if you ask me. Should've probably done that first. I keep telling her not to worry. After all the shit that I've been through the last few weeks, I'm pretty sure that there's nothing out on that course that can hurt me. Kutty is nervous too. His payment depends on me doing this shit, perfectly. I know Slick-Willie's nervous 'cause all his "friends" and "associates" will be watching and judging him. And now I'm starting to freak-out because, everyone else's shit depends on me. And, as if all that isn't enough, here comes The Specialist.

The Specialist - "Mr. Gem, Mr. Kutner; would you please come with me? I have made a couple changes I would like you to see."

Gem - "Sauer-boy, you look different. Did you just get your eyebrows done? Really, it looks good. Like you're even more angry than usual."

The Specialist - "Oh, thank you. I was afraid it may be too much."

Gem - "No, it suits you."

He walks us to the end of the course. There, sitting inside an open WWII style jeep, are two dead pigs.

Kutty - "Are we having a luau?"

The Specialist - "No. This is my addition to the end of the show. When you finish with the building, the door opens, the car will start to drive; like the bad guys are escaping. You chase down the car and cut the pigs open."

By the look on Kutty's bewildered face, I can tell he's thinking what I'm thinking.

Gem - "Dude! What the fuck is wrong with you?!"

The Specialist - "I have seen it done at a weapons demonstration before. The crowd loved it. They stood and cheered."

Gem - "Really? You've actually seen someone do this before?"

The Specialist - "Yes, only they used explosives and dead chickens."

Gem - "Chickens?"

The Specialist - "Chickens."

Gem - "Chickens."

The Specialist - "Yeah, chickens!"

Gem - "You have a fucked-up circle of friends. And I don't know about this. Let me think about it for a minute."

The Specialist - "Gem, this is very important to me. Please consider that while you are thinking it over."

Why would he tell me that? All it did was give me even more leverage. I go back to the lab to think things over. Kutty and The Specialist follow me in. I'm not really worried about the pigs out there. I'm more concerned with how to ease everyone's tensions, especially mine.

Gem - "So, your entire compensation depends on my performance today?"

Kutty - "Yep."

Gem - "I still can't believe you did an all-or-nothing deal. My eight-year-old, would've told you not to sign that contract. A contract isn't something to be entered into lightly. It has to be built, then massaged and contorted, to benefit all parties involved. You have to study your adversary, find out what's important to them and then show them that the only way they're going to get what they want, is to give you what you want. Observe..."

[Gem yells out to The Specialist, who is sitting anxiously in his office.]

Gem - "Hey man-doll! Go tell Willie I'm not doing this shit."

He didn't even say anything. He just looked confused and ran-off to tell Willie.

Gem - "You guys might want to take some notes because, there's about to be a schoolin'."

About a minute later, Sauer returns with Willie. The freaked-out looks on their faces were priceless.

Willie - "What is the problem here, Mr. Gem? It's a couple of things added to the program. I expect you will still perform your end of the bargain."

Oh really bitch?

Gem - "Listen-up, Willie. That, out there, wasn't part of the bargain. If fact, no part of this whole, fucking, freak-show was part of the fucking bargain. So, don't try to throw that shit in my face. I agreed to do this because, I felt you've been fair with me. Now, I'm not so sure anymore. You know how disgusting I think that kind of shit is yet, you had no problem putting me into this situation. How would you feel?"

Willie - "You're right Mr. Gem. I am the one asking you to go beyond the scope of our agreement. What say, I sweeten the offer? How about a hundred-ounce gold bar?"

Gem - "No way man! It's not the money. Those things are nasty to begin with, and God only knows how long they've been rotting for. Just the thought of it is making me puke a little."

Willie - "Two bars."

Gem - "Are you not understanding me?"

Willie - "Three!"

Gem - "Deal!"

Willie - "Will your nausea be at bay?"

Gem - "I'll find a way to deal with it."

Willie - "See, Mr. Gem, it's always about the money."

Gem - "Yeah, speaking of that, you'd better bring them now. Wouldn't want us to waste valuable rehearsal time."

Willie sends Sauer to fetch the gold bars. Then looks at me, nervously.

Willie - "There is one other matter I'd like to discuss, while we have a moment."

Gem - "What's that Willie?"

Willie - "Well, that's just it. I don't particularly like being called...Willie."

Oh my God! It sounds even better when he says it.

Gem - "Wilhelm just sounds too sinister to me and I'm not about to call you mister anything. So, it's either Willie or you can take a pick from some of the other names, that I call you behind your back. But believe me, you're not going to like any of them better than Willie."

Willie - "If you know it bothers me, why do you continue to do it?"

Gem - "I don't know. I guess it's because I know it bothers you. Maybe I'm like a kid that way?"

Kutty - "In more ways than that."

Gem - "Shut-it, Kutty. You're supposed to be taking notes."

Willie - "Getting back to my point; I would appreciate, very much, if you would refrain from calling me 'Willie' in front of our guest."

Gem - "Look, I get it. You're trying to impress these people and me calling you Willie may be perceived as a sign of disrespect, by those who are not familiar with our friendly banter."

Willie - "I couldn't have said it better myself."

Gem - "Well, today is your day Willie. And if me not calling Willie 'Willie', is what Willie wants then, today, being Willie's day, that's what Willie gets."

[Willie looks confused. Sauer comes back with five gold bars. Willie looks at him, now even more confused.]

The Specialist - "I brought extras in case the negotiations weren't going well."

Willie - "I think three will do. Mr. Gem and I have come to an agreement."

Gem - "Don't put those away. I'll get them from you by the end of the night."

Willie - "Am I to expect more surprises?"

Gem - "No. They're going to be my bonus."

Willie - "Just don't disappoint me."

Gem - "Don't you worry. It's gonna be graceful, violent and end with a bang. Your peeps will love it."

Willie - "Thank you, Mr. Gem."

Gem - "Enjoy your party, Mr. Dietrich."

Willie smiled proudly, as he walked away. He actually thought it was a victory. Fuck it. Let him have his day. Sauer hands me the gold bars.

The Specialist - "If you don't mind, we have much to go over."

Gem - "I'll be out in a minute."

Great! Now that I got what I needed, it's time to pep-up my crew. I drop the first bar on the table, in front of Kutty.

Gem - "Enjoy your retirement house."

I drop the next one on the table, in front of Lana.

Gem - "Tell David to enjoy his college education."

They're both looking at me in amazement.

Kutty - "Jesus! What's this thing worth?"

Gem - "Look-up the price of gold and multiply it by 100."

Kutty checks the spot price of gold on his phone.

Kutty - "Holy crap! That's more than I was getting for this whole deal."

Lana - "Are you crazy?"

Gem - "Some would say so but, not this time. This time, I'm just doing the right thing and taking care of my team. Feel better now?"

Kutty - "Thank you, Gem."

He hugged me. I thought he was about to cry. Then Lana actually does. She hugs me too.

Lana - "Thank you, Gem."

Gem - "See, what'd I tell you? I'm an acquired taste."

Lana - "Don't you ever change your flavor."

Gem - "Okay, I think we've jerked each other off long enough. We've got work to do."

Kutty and I go back out to the course. Sauer is explaining his plan but, I've got my own. And it's gonna be awesome!

****

[It's Showtime.]

It's ten minutes before the show. I ask everyone to leave the lab so, I have some time to get dressed and clear my mind.

Kutty - "You're gonna do great. See you out there."

Gem - "Thanks, Kutty."

Lana - "Any last-minute requests?"

Gem - "Not unless you happen to have a cheerleader outfit and a pair of pompoms on you."

She just smiles, gives me a hug and walks out. I think she thought I was kidding. The guards leave the lab too. Now, it's just me and my thoughts. Not always a desirable combination but, today, it's about focus and what Kutty calls "situational awareness". I brought a picture with me for motivation. It's of me and the boys in our lab coats, ready to make our first batch of our colloid. It seems so long ago. God I miss them.

I get dressed. Black t-shirt, black Kung-Fu pants and a black boxing robe, which I had fitted with an extra-large, loose hood to give it a Grim Reaper look. Everything is black to add to the contrast with the silver. Two shortened scythes cross my back. I don't plan on using them, they're mostly there for effect. And finally, I turn my face into a silver mask, which I plan to keep-on as long as there are "guests" around. Mostly for anonymity purposes but, also 'cause it looks freaken' cool.

[There's a knock on the door. Gem opens it, it's Kutty.]

Kutty - "You ready?"

Gem - "As ready as I'm gonna be. Let's do this shit."

Kutty goes out first and signals that we're good to go. The music starts; that's my cue. As I walk out, I look at the crowd seated on the terrace. They're all dressed up, like they're at an opera, or something. There's gotta be well over a hundred people up there. I walk up to my starting point, listen for my cue in the song and...go!

[Gem starts running the course. Jumping, bending, stretching, contorting. Going over, under, through any and all obstacles. He hits his targets and avoids everything that tries to hit him. He is flawless. He gets to the top of the warped wall and grabs-on to the polls.]

That first part was easy. We practiced it so much, I could have done that shit with my eyes closed.

[He hears his cue in the song and sling-shots himself. Forming his arms into wings, he's flying towards the tower.]

The original plan was for me to smash through the roof and punch, slice and stab the dummy-guards inside. I thought I'd add a little more drama to that.

[Gem tucks his wings, forms into a projectile and smashes through the glass on the forth floor, shoulder-rolls, jumps and proceeds to demolish everything.]

I'm busting through walls, grabbing on to ledges, swinging myself to various floors, criss-crossing the entire building and smashing through every piece of glass I see. I stretch-bend around corners, grabbing whatever's there and flinging it out. Bodies of the dummies are flying everywhere. I knock-out the security system with a hammer-blow, sending it flying through a wall and to the ground. Short-out the communications equipment, sparks abound. Tear through the command center, while dismembering every dummy there, with my chopping move. And free the hostages, on the ground floor. I hear the garage door opening, the little jeep with the pigs begins to move. I know I'm supposed to chase it down but, this is where I improvise, again. I swing myself to the roof of the tower. The crowd is totally into it. They're pointing and yelling that the pigs are getting away. I pretend that I just noticed it too. I run off the ledge with my arms out / lose momentum and begin to fall / tuck into a dive position / turn my arms into wings, feet into a tail, and pull-up right before I hit the ground. As I fly over the swine, I turn my arms into spears / stab them both through their heads and into their bodies / do a half-roll when I hit the ground / yank them out of the vehicle / fling them out / morph my hands into spheres inside them / quickly expand the spheres / and with a couple of loud booms, blow those poor bastards to smithereens. Chunks of pig rain down on the course. The crowd's on it's feet; they're lovin' it! But I'm not done, yet. While still on my ass, I turn towards the jeep and extend my legs out, as hard and as fast as I can. I slam the fucking thing and send it flying into the second story of the building. The tower collapses onto its side, breaking into pieces (told-ya the thing was flimsy). The crowd goes ballistic! What a bunch of fucking freaks.

    I get-up and start walking towards the on-lookers, with purpose; proud of how bad-ass I just was. The crowd is pouring down the terrace stairs, still clapping, tripping over each-other. I pull-out a hand towel and a bottle of hand sanitizer, I had stashed in my "suit" and give my arms a quick once-over, before I reach my fans. Everybody's ecstatic; Kutty's pumping his fists in the air, Willie's ear-to-ear smiles and even Lana's jumping up and down and clapping. I'm seeing her in slow-motion, I wish she actually did have that cheerleader outfit on. It would have gone great with that bounce.

[Gem walks through the crowd and into the mansion, to clean-up.]

****

[After the show.]

The terrace looks beautiful. Music playing, food and drinks galore, everybody seems to be having a good time. Willie's got a group of dinos and douche-bags around him; congratulating, shaking hands, patting him on the back. Oddly, I don't see anyone from Lockhart here. I guess he thinks he's all the representation they need. Sauer is running around making sure every-thing's right. I decide to work the crowd. It's probably a good idea to know who these people are. Some may be of future benefit others, potential problems. As soon as they see me, all the "guests" swarm around me. They all want a piece of me. The dinos and douche-bags are bragging about themselves and their companies. Handing me their cards, asking me to come work for them. What a bunch of assholes. They're at Willie's party, trying to steal his "find". Their "significant others" were a perfect fit for their back-stabbing nature. They were handing me their numbers too only, for a different reason. They wanted to see what else I can morph and stretch.

I'm ten minutes into my excursion with these "people", and I'm already looking for a way out. And I know just how to do it. I make my way to the music stage and pick up the microphone. The music stops and all eyes are on me.

Gem - "Good evening. Thank you all for coming and for all the compliments and the generous offerings. I would like to say a couple of things about our host, Mr. Wilhelm Dietrich. Now, I have to be honest with you, when I first met Mr. Dietrich, I wasn't too impressed. In fact, I believe my exact thoughts were, 'what a pompous douche-bag'. But I have come to see him otherwise. He brought me in, helped me financially, explained why I shouldn't keep my abilities secret, how we can achieve a greater good and put together an amazing team to help develop my skills. And, through it all, he's been nothing less then accommodating, patient and very generous. Tomorrow morning, I will be performing a never before done surgery, on a little boy with an inoperable brain tumor. Mr. Dietrich was instrumental in setting that up as well. So sadly, I must leave; I have to get my rest. But before I do, I would like to raise my glass to Mr. Wilhelm Dietrich. May the legacy of your vision, intellect and generosity, live long after we're all pushing daisies.

[The guests applaud and sip their drinks.]

Gem - "Oh, crap. I almost forgot...Mr. Sebastian Sauer. When I first met him, Mr. Dietrich said that he calls him 'The Specialist'. I believe my exact thoughts were, 'oh great, another douche-bag'. I was wrong again. This man is one of the smartest, hardest working, creative and loyal people, I've ever met. Without him, the entire show would have probably consisted of me breaking a couple of dummies and climbing up a wall or two. He not only planned this show, he also came up with ideas for the impossible surgery to help make it a reality. So, let's raise our glasses to "The Specialist ". A man who has truly earned his title.

I drink the drink and start heading out. Quickly shaking the hands that are flying towards me, till I get to Willie's. I look him in the eye, give him a firm handshake and a big hug. I don't know if he's ever been this happy, in his life.

Willie - "You truly are a Gem."

Gem - "That's what I've been trying to tell you! There's always a price to pay to have me around. But I'm worth it. Hey, where's your boy?"

Willie - "He said he will meet you out front. I think you have struck a chord with him. I have never seen him emotional before. But I can't say I blame him."

Gem - "Yeah, I seem to have that effect on people."

[Willie pats Gem on the back and goes back to his guests. Gem walks to the front of the house and sees Mr. Sauer pulling his car up. Sauer gets out of the car, looks at Gem and smiles.]

Gem - "Valets too busy?"

The Specialist - "I wanted to do it myself. Thank for all the kind words."

Gem - "You earned them."

He looks at me as if I were a hero but, I haven't earned that yet. I get into the car and notice something on the passenger seat; the two gold bars, my bonus. These, I earned.

****

[Day 13]

[Wednesday. Day of the surgery. 7:30 AM]

Natasha and I are having breakfast in the boys' hospital room. Lana comes in, she spent the night with her son. She's having second thoughts about the surgery.

Lana - "I feel like we're missing something. What if I forgot to teach you something? What if..."

Gem - "Okay, let me ask you this...what if we skip the surgery today? What if we don't get another chance to do this?"

She's just looking at me. I know she's afraid. Who wouldn't be? I'd be freaking out too. I need to try a different approach to calming her down because, a nervous Lana will be pretty useless in this situation.

Gem - "Lana, I know you're scared. But you can't let the fear get to you. I know what you're feeling; it's a sad, cold, dark place to be. You can't stay there. Sure, you can hang out for a bit; do a little crying, some blaming, maybe even some self-pitying but, then, you gotta get the fuck out. Because, your situation isn't gonna fix itself. So, get-up, focus and we're going to do this like I know we can."

Lana - "How are you so calm?"

Gem - "I've had a lot of practice and a great teacher. I know I'm ready."

[Lana kisses Gem on the cheek, hugs Natasha and leaves to finish prepping.]

Gem Thinks - "Shit! Now I'm nervous too. What if we did miss something?"

Natasha - "You should probably go too. The surgery is in an hour and you need to get ready. And don't you start worrying too. I know you can do this."

[Natasha gives Gem a kiss and he goes to get prepared for the operation.]

[10:00 AM]

I am sanitized and ready to go. I enter the operating room, everybody's already there. Willie and his "associates" are looking down from the viewing balcony. He smiles when he sees me and gives me a thumbs-up. Must be residual happiness from yesterday. Lana's back to normal; focused and in control. I walk up to the table, place my hand into a heavy metal block, that Kutty designed to keep my hand perfectly still during the procedure, look at Lana, take a deep breath...and we begin.

I make the incision; it feels much softer and warmer than what I've been working with. I can see everything I'm doing on a screen in front of me. Lana's directing me around sensitive areas (which is pretty much all of them), till we finally get to the mass. It feels different from the surrounding tissue, which is good because, now I don't have to rely on the ultrasound, I can do it by feel. That means less chance of missing something. I turn my probe into a tube. They hook me up to the ultrasonic generator and adjust the frequency until the mass starts to "liquefy". They place a suction device on the other opening I made and proceed to vacuum out the tumor. I feel around a bit to make sure we got it all and then begin to retract the probe. That's when fate decided to throw me another curve-ball.

[Alarms go off / David's vitals are dropping.]

Gem - "What's going on? What happened?"

Nobody's answering. They're trying to figure it out. I feel something, there's more liquid. Fuck! I must have snagged a blood vessel on the way out.

Gem - "I hit a blood vessel! Find it!"

Lana - "There!"

I see it on the screen. I reconnect the vessel, by making a tube between the two ends.

Gem - "I got it!"

David's vitals are getting better. The blood flow has been reestablished. But now we have to cauterize. I can do this but, then I have to show the one ability I've been hiding from these assholes. Lana knows it too. She's looking at me with desperate eyes. Fuck it! I'm not about to let this kid die for that.

[Gem extends his other hand towards Lana.]

Gem - "Plug me in."

[Lana hesitates. Everyone else in the room looks confused.]

Gem - "Fuckin' plug me in!"

She's hesitating because she knows I don't want to do it. She also knows, we don't have a choice. This was it; the "something" we didn't plan for but, should have.

[Lana takes Gem's outstretched hand and places it in front of an outlet, he plugs-in. Gem cauterizes the blood vessel. All signs are good.]

I look at Lana, she's relieved but, has a guilty, apologetic look on her face. I look over at the audience and everyone is happy; shaking Willie's hand, patting him on the back. Willie's looking back at me. He's smiling too, except his is more of an "Ah-ha!", smile. He knows how big this is. As for me, I'm feeling a bit queasy, flush and like I'm gonna throw-the-fuck-up. I quickly head to the prep room and hunch over a big sink. Lana comes in right behind me.

Lana - "Thank you so much! I'm sorry I ever doubted you."

Gem - "No problem."

Lana - "The mass was benign."

I lift my head and look at her happy face. I want to tell her that I'm happy for them but, when I open my mouth, it's not words that come out; it's my breakfast. I turn my head back towards the sink, as fast as I can.

Gem - "Sorry, did I get you?"

I look over at her. Yeah...I got her. She's not dripping in it but, let's just say, it's a good thing she wears glasses and too bad she took the head covering off. She takes off her glasses, (so she can see) and hugs me.

Gem - "Look at you. You're covered in my breakfast and you still want to hug me...acquired taste."

Lana - "I'm sorry...that should have been something obvious to plan for. I fucked-up."

Gem - "We both did. But today is not about that. Today is about your little one, getting a second chance. It's about your family getting a second chance. Go enjoy it. Let me worry about the Will-ster."

[Lana starts to walk out.]

Gem - "Uhhh...you might wanna wash-up first. You got a little...pretty much everywhere, except your back."

I get cleaned-up, change my clothes and go back to Natasha and the boys. I feel good about what I did and who knows, maybe karma will throw me a little bone for it.

****

I walk into the room and see Willie standing there, speaking with Natasha; telling her how "amazing" I am. Stupid karma. I asked for a little bone and it gives me a fucking dildo.

Willie - "Mr. Gem! I was just telling your lovely wife, how amazed we all are by you. Both, as a person and in your ever-evolving abilities."

Gem - "Thank you for the compliments but, can we do this another time? I just got done with a nerve-wracking, three-hour surgical procedure, after which I dumped my breakfast on Lana."

Natasha - "Ewww!"

Gem - "Yeah, it was pretty gross...and funny."

Willie - "What we have seen displayed by you, has been nothing short of miraculous. In light of that and the new skills you've developed, my associates and I, feel that more time is required for our research. As for compensation, you make a list and consider it done."

Gem - "What-ever I want?"

Willie - "Anything you want."

Gem - "Let me think about it. I will give you an answer tomorrow."

Willie - "I understand, Mr. Gem. Please, take some time to unwind; think it through on a clear mind. I will give the team, a well-deserved day off tomorrow. We can reconvene on Friday."

Gem - "Thanks for understanding."

[They shake hands, say their good-byes and Willie leaves. Gem and Natasha discuss Willie's offer.]

CHAPTER SIX:

GAMES ARE OVER

[Day 14: Thursday, 7:45 AM]

I arrive at the mansion. I know Willie gave us the day off but, I wanted to talk to him about his proposal. What the hell is this? What are all these hazmat cleanup trucks doing here? Did the party get out of control after I left? Oh no, I hope nothing happened to the lab.

[Gem walks around back to the lab entrance. He sees people in hazmat suits, taking things out in large, black, rubber bags. He runs into the lab.]

I go into the lab. Everything looks fine. Then, I notice that the hazmat guys are going through Sauer-boy's office. I walk in and see a side door I've never noticed before. I look in; it's another fuckin' lab. Only, this one is huge. As I walk through, I see several glass rooms, all of which had clean-up underway. There's blood everywhere; body parts coated with or made-of various types of metals. It looks like they exploded or burned off of their bodies. That's what's being cleaned and loaded into the rubber bags.

[The Specialist walks in.]

The Specialist - "Mr. Gem, I believe you've ventured into the wrong part of the lab."

Gem - "Oh, you think so? What the fuck is this?!"

[The Specialist starts to escort Gem out. Gem keeps looking back at the carnage as he's walking out.]

The Specialist - "I was told that you had the day off."

Gem - "I did. I just came to speak with Willie about his offer. Now, please explain to me; what the fuck did I just see in there?"

[The Specialist looks concerned. Gem wasn't supposed to know about the other lab or what was going-on in there.]

The Specialist - "It was experimentation for an unrelated project."

Gem - "Unrelated, huh? It looks pretty, fucking related to me!"

The Specialist - "I am sorry, Gem. I'm afraid I don't have any answers for you. Perhaps it would be best if you came back tomorrow, when Mr. Dietrich is back."

Gem - "Yes, perhaps it would be."

[Gem gets in his car and heads back to the hospital. He is in disbelief.]

I knew they'd eventually try to duplicate me but, I can't believe the lengths they went to. They rushed it and killed people. And the saddest part is, they don't even give a shit. I am so done with these assholes.

[Gem arrives at the boys' room. Victor is there, having tea with Natasha.]

Victor - "There he is, our Gem, miracle worker."

Natasha - "So, how did it go?"

Gem - "Willie was out. I'll have to see him tomorrow."

Natasha - "What's wrong? Why do you look so, anxious?"

Gem - "Oh, it's nothing. Just wanted to get things wrapped-up today."

Natasha - "It's okay. Relax, enjoy your break. I'm going to leave you two to catch-up."

Gem - "Where are you going?"

Natasha - "Well, I haven't been home in two days; I'm going to shower, change and come right back. Keys please."

Gem - "Victor, would you mind taking her? I want to keep my car here; in case I need it."

Victor - "My pleasure. I always have time for beautiful woman."

[Natasha kisses Gem and walks out. Victor begins to follow but, Gem stops him.]

Gem - "Keep an eye out."

Victor - "Why? What's happening?"

Gem - "I saw something today that's making me think that things are about to get a lot less cordial, between me and Willie."

Victor - "Yes, I've been wanting to tell you; I got intel back on him yesterday. Gem, these guys are dangerous. They are very well-connected organization with shit-load of money."

Gem - "You'll have to tell me later. Go before Natasha gets curious."

[Victor nods his head and leaves with Natasha. Gem sits on a chair, across from the boys and assesses the situation. He knows the craziness is just beginning.]

****

[Victor and Natasha are driving to Natasha's house.]

Natasha - "Did you notice Gem acting a little weird?"

Victor - "It's Gem, he's always a little weird."

Natasha - "Yeah but, just now, he was weirder than usual."

Victor - "Right now, inside, Gem is dying. You and boys are everything for him. You are his heart, his happiness. You bring out his good side. His happy side. You think you know Gem because you know his sides?

His funny side, crazy side, smart side, doing stupid things with boys side; even when he get mad and scream little bit, all good sides. But there is other side of Gem. Very mean, crazy, sadistic, sarcastic-asshole side."

Natasha - "Gem?"

Victor - "Yes."

Natasha - "Mean and sadistic?"

Victor - "Yes."

Natasha - "Yeah, right! Gem felt bad about killing a mouse once. He doesn't like violence or seeing things suffer."

Victor - "That is exactly why he gets that way. Because he hates to see suffering, he hates injustice. Do you know who give him name Gem? Me. Why? Not because why you think. Not because he has all different sides like a gemstone. Not because he is so valuable like diamond but, because he is typical, fucking Gemini. He really only has two sides. The good side and the scary-asshole side. And when the asshole side come out, he become another person; gruesome, mean, crazy but, very fun to watch."

Natasha - "Gem doesn't have a 'scary-asshole' side. Although, he can be an asshole sometimes."

Victor - "You think you see his asshole side? What you have seen, is just a little piece of ass, not even the hole. That what you know as asshole, is not even close to what I'm talking about. Me and Gem have long history together, before you meet him. Did he ever tell you how we meet?"

Natasha - "You know, now that you've mentioned it, no. I can't believe I never thought to ask him about that. Is it an interesting story?"

Victor - "One day, when everything back to normal and I am certain that he is stable, I will tell you."

Natasha - "I can't believe it! Mr. KGB Tough-Guy, is scared of Gem."

Victor - "Do you know story of food-box."

Natasha - "Food-box?"

Victor - "You know, that metal food-box, the one with pictures of girls on it."

Natasha - "Oh, you mean the 'Charlie's Angels' lunch box?"

Victor - "Yes, that."

Natasha - "Yeah, he told me he got it because, he thought it'd be cool to have a lunch box with pretty girls on it. And one day, he used it to beat-up some bullies. He says he keeps it to remind himself of that day.

There's a picture inside of him with the swat-team. He's all bruised-up but, smiling. He says it was his defining moment. The day he discovered his inner strength."

Victor - "That is watered-down version of the story. Those bullies, were teenage dope-dealers. They beat Gem and his friend because they wouldn't leave playground. Gem call police but, next day, dope-dealers back. Next day, Gem go back to playground. One hand, lunch box full with rocks; other hand, shortened hockey stick. He beat them until they unconscious. Then, he gets other kids from neighborhood. They make weapons from garden tools, go back to playground wait for dope-dealer's boss. When he comes, he comes with others. Gem leads other kids to attack. Boss pulls out gun, gets-off one shot. The rocks in Gem's food-box stop the bullet. When Gem and others get bad guys, they almost kill them. The police in picture were there to stop them. Gem was proud that he make justice. He even write it on box; 'justice' in his blood, before he gets them. 'Served' in blood of dope-boss, after he gets them. And this, when he was only a boy."

Natasha - "Um...okay, that's an interesting story."

[They pull up to the house. Victor notices a car park a couple of houses down but, no one is getting out.]

Victor - "You go do what you need to do. I am going to stay out here. I have a few calls to make."

Natasha - "Okay, I'll try to make it quick."

Victor - "Take your time. I'll be here."

[Natasha heads into the house. She sees the lunch box on the mantle; it looks somewhat different now. Victor stays in his car, watching the other car. He takes a few pictures of it.]

[30 minutes later, Natasha gets back in the car.]

Victor - "Wow! Only thirty minutes for everything. You should teach classes to other wives."

[They drive off. Victor sneaks a video of the car and its two male occupants.]

Victor - "I hope the story I tell you, doesn't make you see Gem in bad way."

Natasha - "No, I liked the story. I've seen him argue thousands of times and get into a couple of scuffles but, nothing like that. It's oddly comforting for me to know that he's capable of such 'justice serving'."

Victor - "I am happy that you're not upset about it."

Natasha - "Why would I be upset? I'm proud of him for it. Vic, tell me the story of how you met."

[Victor looks at the rear-view mirror. The car is following them again. He reluctantly decides to tell Natasha the story.]

Victor - "When we met, I was drinking a lot. I was in depression and wanting to just die. I bring my family here, no money, no job, no nothing. It was hard for me to find work because of my years with KGB. One night, I drink too much, I get in fight. They start to beat me. Gem, comes and says to them, 'Leave him. I take care of this asshole myself.' Now, I knew Gem a little from before; nice, funny…a little crazy but, I did not expect what will happen next. I look at him from the floor, he helps me up, I say 'thank you'. He look at me, shake his head and say, 'don't thank me yet.', and he smashes bottle on my head. I pass out. I wake up, tied to metal post, in abandoned building, Gem standing in front of me. I was in standing position, legs tied, waist tied, hands tied, everything tied to post. Gem say to me, 'I can see you don't really give a shit about living so, I'm gonna help you out'. I ask him if he is going to kill me. He say, 'We'll see but, first I am going to put you through the same hell that your suicidal-bullshit is putting your family through. You have a good wife and a sweet, innocent, little boy at home. You are breaking them and you don't care. Today I will show you what that pain feels like.' He steps aside, I see tools...power tools; saws, knives, blowtorch. I say 'why you doing this?'. He say, 'Because, I won't let you take the easy way out'. I had no doubt that he was intending to use everything there to punish me. I beg him, 'Please! Don't do this!' He say, 'Did you give your family a choice? No. Then why do you deserve one?' I had no answer. He picked-up a sledgehammer and says, 'We'll just start at the feet and work our way up.' I see the look in his eyes, it was angry, happy and indifferent all at same time. First time in my life I was so scared. I cry, beg him, what can I do? He say, 'You already did. Now, it's my turn to do.' He lifts up hammer, I scream, 'Please, I don't want to die! I want to fix it!' He come right to my face, look in his eyes still same, crazy like before. Then, his face changes from crazy to just serious and he said to me, 'Then go be a man to your family.' He untie me. I say, 'thank you.' I want to hug him but he push me away and says, 'clean up first.' I look down and my pants are wet. I was so scared of this maniac that I piss my pants. Then he looks at me and says, 'I'm hungry. You want to get a burger? Don't worry, we'll do the drive-thru. You can sit on the tarp so, you don't mess-up my car.' Crazy fucking bastard. Next day, he come to my house and take me to find job. And that's how we become friends. I owe everything to him."

[Natasha looks bewildered.]

Natasha - "Gem?"

Victor - "Yes! Fucking Gemini."

Natasha - "So, why after all these years, are you telling me this story now?"

Victor - "Because Gem has very strong sense of justice and to him, you and children are the innocent. And because, I have feeling that he is close to snapping. He feels frustrated, guilty for everything that happened, he is miserable without his kids. The only thing missing from this shit-cocktail, is his anger. And, I am getting the feeling that someone is about to pour that in too."

[Victor looks in the rear-view mirror again. Natasha sees him and looks back at the car behind them.]

Natasha - "Who are they?"

Victor - "I'm not sure but, I'm sure we will find out."

[Victor and Natasha get back to the hospital. Victor shows Gem the pictures and video of the car that followed them. Gem confirms that they are

Willie's guys. He tells Victor and Natasha what he saw at the mansion. They talk things over and decide to see how Gem's meeting with Willie will go, before doing anything drastic. Victor will come and stay with Natasha and the boys, while Gem is out.]

****

[Day 15]

[Friday, 7:45 AM]

I arrive at the mansion for what is hopefully, the last time ever. I walk in through the back, as usual, and into the lab. Everything looks all cleaned-up. Lana and Kutty aren't in yet. Sauer-boy comes in and tells me that Willie wants to meet with me in his study. I pull out my phone and turn on the voice recorder. Here we go.

[Gem and The Specialist walk into the study. Willie is there to greet them.]

Willie - "Ah, Mr. Gem. Please have a seat."

[Gem sits in a chair that's closest to Willie.]

Willie - "First, I would like to thank you again, for the amazing show and incredible surgery you performed."

Gem - "It was my pleasure. When I feel like someone went out of their way to be fair and honest with me, I try to do the same for them."

Willie - "Are you implying that, up-to that point, that was the only time you felt that I was being fair and honest with you?"

Gem - "I'm not implying anything, Willie. I'm flat out telling you; that was the only time. Don't get me wrong, compensation wise, you've been above and beyond fair. It's the 'honest' part we're missing here. 'Cause, after what I saw here yesterday, I'm pretty sure you haven't been 'honest' about your intentions."

Willie - "If I may ask, why did you choose to keep the electrical aspect a secret?"

Gem - "Because I knew it'd be weaponized."

Willie - "With the surgery, you've shown that it could be used otherwise."

Gem - "And with all the dismembered bodies I saw, you've shown me that it wouldn't."

Willie - "My associates and I are very excited, about the prospect of having you with us, for further study. Have you made a decision?"

Gem - "Yes. And it's, no."

Willie - "I told you that money is no object. After all the new business we've attracted, we have the entire organization backing us now. Name your price, any price."

Shit! He's heading back towards desperation, again. And like I said before, I don't like to see these kinds of assholes desperate. They become too dangerous.

Gem - "This time, it's really not about the money. I'm out."

Willie - "I sincerely hope you reconsider the offer."

Gem - "We agreed on three weeks from the beginning."

Willie - "You are right. That was our agreement. But, only because you left me with no other option. And I was mistakenly certain that within three weeks, I could help you see things from my perspective."

Gem - "Sorry Willie. I guess I just can't get my head far enough up my ass, to see things from your perspective."

Willie - "I see. Let me put it another way; your performance has attracted a lot of attention from my associates. To let you go now, before we have completed our project, would be detrimental, for both of us. These are the people who decide who gets what, in our organization. In fact, it's thanks to them that I am Chairman and CEO of Lockhart Industries. And thanks to them, that we met."

Gem - "So, I guess Mr. Lockhart's unexpected death, was a pretty lucky coincidence for you."

Willie - "Mr. Gem, men like me, men of great vision and ambition, cannot afford to leave their dreams in the hands of 'lucky coincidences'. We make our own fortunes. We see what we want, pull the strings and we make it happen. Masters of our own destiny."

Gem Thinks - "Oh my God! This sack-of-shit killed Mr. Lockhart!"

Gem - "And the collateral damage? The death, the suffering, the, God only knows what the fuck you guys did down there?"

Willie - "Those men volunteered. After the show, it wasn't hard to find those who wished to be like you. Unfortunately, due to time constraints, we had to experiment much more than I would have liked to. Then, we find out there's more to you than we even dreamed of. I'm afraid, at this point, there isn't any choice but, to continue the research."

Gem - "Are you threatening me? Were you not privy to the events that unfolded before your very eyes, the past few days? Don't fuck with me, Willie. Or I will put on a show that will leave you breathless, literally."

Willie - "I wouldn't dream of 'fucking' with you, Mr. Gem. I know you can handle yourself. But there are those around you, who are infinitely more vulnerable than you and you can't be everywhere at once."

[Gem stands up and comes right-up to Willie.]

Gem - "If you ever threaten my family again; what I did to those pigs will seem like child's play."

[Gem walks out of the mansion and gets into his car.]

God fuckin' damn-it! Now, the powers that make me extra-awesome, have made my loved ones targets. I thought they used this premise in so many stories because, the writers were getting lazy. But much to my chagrin, that's exactly what's happened.

[Gem starts his car. He hears another loud noise. It's Willie's helicopter taking off.]

Gem Thinks - "Oh-no! No, no, no!"

CHAPTER SEVEN:

THINGS TAKE A TWIST

[Gem sees the helicopter taking off. It's headed in the direction of the hospital.]

Gem Thinks - "Shit! This fucker isn't wasting any time."

[Gem calls Natasha / no answer.]

Gem - "Fuck! Why does she always leave it on vibrate? What, she's afraid the ringer might wake the kids? I'm pretty sure that would be a good thing, right about now!"

[Gem dials Victor.]

Gem - "Come on you commi-bastard."

[Victor answers his phone.]

Victor - "Gem, how did meeting with asshole go?"

Gem - "Vic, are you with Natasha?"

Victor - "I just go to get cappuccino for her from cafeteria. I'm going back now."

Gem - "Victor, get back to Natasha and hide her. Then stay with the boys, I'll be there soon."

Victor - "Meeting went bad?"

Gem - "Meeting went fucked! He threatened me, I threatened him, and now they're on their way to the hospital, in a fuckin' helicopter!"

Victor - "Why the fuck you warn him. If someone threaten you, you don't say I get you next time, you get him this time. Warning only gives them time to fuck you more."

Gem - "Victor, when I get a time-machine, then you can tell me what I should have done. For now, please, go take care of my family."

Victor - "I take care of it. Will be back in room in one minute."

Gem - "Please Vic, if anything happens to them, I'm gonna lose it. Victor? Victor!"

[The line went dead. Gem tries to call Natasha again. No answer.]

Gem - "God damn-it! Why even have a phone, if you never pick it up?!"

[A few minutes later, Gem gets back to the hospital. He stops his car out front and runs in. He gets to the boys' room. Boys still there; Natasha and Victor are not. Gem runs to the roof, where the landing pad is; the helicopter is gone. He runs back to the room. There's a note on the table. It says, "8:00 AM tomorrow. Location to follow." Gem collapses into a chair.]

Gem Thinks - "How the fuck did I let this happen? Victor was right. I should've killed them when I had the chance. Now, they have leverage and that puts them in control."

[Gem sits and thinks about what to do next.]

Gem Thinks - "Why do they need till tomorrow morning? What are they planning for me and mine? I highly doubt that Willie will just let them go, even if he gets me. No, we're in way-too-fucking deep for that to happen."

[Gem looks at his sons.]

Gem Thinks - "Will they be next?"

[He looks at the pictures Natasha set-up next to the boy's beds. One of them, is of the boys holding Gem's lunch box.]

I told them the real story of what happened that day. They were so excited when I let them hold that lunch box in their little hands.

[Gem stares at the picture for a moment.]

Gem Thinks - "Fuck this! I'm going preemptive on those motherfuckers! I didn't almost die as a kid, to be a pussy now!"

[Gem leaves the hospital, looks for his car, it's been towed. He looks around and sees the car of the men who were following Natasha and Victor. They're not in it.]

Gem Thinks - "I wonder if they're still inside or if they left on the helicopter."

[He walks back in. He sees them watching him, from a hallway near the lobby. He walks up to them.]

Willie's Guy 1 - "Leaving so soon? Your appointment isn't till tomorrow morning."

Gem - "You two snowballers really crossed the line. Where are they?"

Willie's Guy 2 - "Don't worry, you will find out soon enough. For now, why don't you just go back to your kids? Who knows how much time you have left together."

[Gem whips out his hands and grabs them both by the balls.]

Gem - "Either of you make a sound and I'm tearing them off."

[Gem looks around for a more private setting. He sees a sign that reads "Orthopedics Equipment Storage". Gem nods them towards the door. They walk in and stand in front of each other.]

Gem - "I don't have much time, which means, neither do you. Start talking."

Willie's Guy 2 - "Or what? What are you gonna do?"

Gem - "Last chance."

Willie's Guy 2 - "I'm not scared of you. You're just a lucky pussy who can't even protect his own fam..."

[SPLAT!!! Gem shots out his hand and smashes him into a wall. The perimeter of the body bursts upon impact. Blood spray, in all directions around the body. Gem and Guy 1 look at the flattened figure.]

Willie's Guy 1 - "Is he dead?"

[The body slowly peels off the wall and falls to the floor, face first.]

Gem - "I think so."

[Gem looks at Guy 1 and smiles.]

Gem - "Your turn."

Willie's Guy 1 - "Please Gem, I'm like you. I have a family too."

Gem - "First of all, you wish you were like me. Second, that didn't stop you from helping them take mine from me."

Willie's Guy 1 - "You're right Gem. I fucked-up. I swear I'm going to quit all this and just have a normal life with my family. Please Gem."

Gem - "Where did they take them?"

Willie's Guy 1 - "They went back to the estate. Mr. Dietrich had his associates leave some of their security people, just in case things didn't go as planned. I also heard them mention a food processing plant but, I don't know what that's about."

Gem - "How many more security guys?"

Willie's Guy 1 - "At least another fifty."

Gem Thinks - "Another fifty, plus Willie's...that's a lot of assholes. "

Gem - "What else you got?"

Willie's Guy 1 - "I also heard Mr. Dietrich tell The Specialist to get the new guns ready."

Gem - "The ones in his safe?"

Willie's Guy 1 "Yes. And Gem, those aren't regular weapons, they called them 'high-particle, energy beam' guns. I swear, that's all I know."

Gem - "I believe that you're being sincere."

Willie's Guy 1 - "So, you won't kill me?"

Gem - "No. But I have to make sure you can't communicate with them."

[Gem, in a fluid motion, breaks his hands...]

Gem - "Can't text."

[...breaks his legs...]

Gem - "Can't walk."

[...breaks his jaw.]

Gem - "Can't talk."

[He looks at Guy 1's passed out body.]

Gem - "Looks like we've covered all the bases."

[Gem washing his hands, thoroughly.]

That wasn't so bad. In fact, I'm excited, I've finally popped my killing cherry. It's quite the liberating experience. Just gotta get the blood off, sanitize a bit and we're good.

[Gem gets their car keys and takes their car. He's on his way to the mansion, thinking about the best course of action.]

Gem Thinks - "Do I sneak in or, just walk in, silver blazing?"

Gem's Conscience - "There has been enough violence already. Those people have families too. You have to try to do this as non-violently as possible."

Gem Thinks - "What the fuck? Is that you, conscience? How nice of you to finally grow a pair and join us. And thanks for the advice but, when has non-violence ever solved anything?"

Gem's Conscience - "You can't go in blazing; your people might get hurt."

Gem Thinks - "And if I go in quietly and they see me, then they'll just use my peeps for leverage. No, I need to create chaos. I want them in panic mode."

Gem's Conscience - "Can you live with the consequences?"

Gem Thinks - "Oh, suck-a-dick, conscience! Where were you when I was telling the boys to get their flippers on?!"

Gem's Conscience - "You can make it worse."

Gem Thinks - "You know what, I'm fucking done with you! You show up, after the fact, and take the fun out of everything."

[Gem waits a second for a response. No response from his conscience.]

Gem - "Yeah, that's what I thought bitch. Max carnage it is."

[Gem arrives at the mansion, calmly walks up to the door and rings the doorbell. One of Willie's guards opens the door.]

Gem - "Good evening, jerk-off. I'm here for my wife, my friend and your salad-tosser boss."

Guard - "I'm afraid that none of the people you mentioned, are available to meet with you right now. We weren't expecting you till tomorrow morning."

Gem - "Yeah, I was kindda hoping to get this all wrapped-up by tomorrow morning."

[Gem sees the foyer filling with guards. All pointing guns at him.]

Gem - "Well, I can see you're busy. I'll just come back another time."

[Gem walks back to the car. The guards start chuckling.]

Don't worry, I didn't puss-out. I just had to make sure that my guys aren't in the foyer. Why?

[He starts the car and drives it right through the doors and into the foyer. Running over a few guards on the way.]

That's why.

[Guard who opened the door is laying on the hood, his head in the windshield. Gem looks at his broken face.]

Gem - "Still funny, bitch?!"

[Gem gets out of the car. All eyes and guns on him. Willie walks onto the loft area, between the two sweeping staircases.]

Willie - "Mr. Gem. It's nice to see you've finally come out of your shell."

Gem - "Shut your shit-dumpster, Willie! You've really crossed into dumb-fuck land with this one. Call-off your ass-monkeys and let's figure this out ourselves. I'm giving you one last chance to..."

[Two armed guards walk Victor and Natasha out to the loft. Gem stretch-jumps towards the loft; he's shot, mid-air with a 50-caliber rifle. He falls to the floor. Natasha gasps. Gem stands up, hole through his abdomen is quickly repairing. Gem looks at the guard who shot him.]

Gem - "Are you sure you want to do this? Did you not see the show? Do you not know what I'm capable of?"

Guard - "We're not a bunch of props that don't fight back. We're trained professionals with high-caliber weapons. Besides, I don't think you have it in you to kill anything."

Gem - "You know, you're the second person to tell me that today, and it didn't work out well for the first guy. And I guess, me driving a car through the fucking front door, didn't quite have the impact I was going for."

Guard - "We'll take our chances."

Gem - "You know, I was really hoping you'd say that."

[Gem throws-out his hand and splats him against a wall.]

Gem Thinks - "I like this move."

[All hell breaks loose. Gem is being shot from every direction. He makes a large shield with his left hand, a scythe with his right and begins his attack. Swinging, jumping, stretching. Chopping, slicing, stabbing, even skewering a few. Blood and body parts, flying everywhere. He hears a thump behind him. He looks down and sees a dead guard with a 50-caliber rifle. Someone shot him before he could shoot Gem.]

Gem Thinks - "Who shot this guy? Was it by accident or do I have a friend here I don't know about?"

[Gem looks around but, there's too much chaos to tell. He sees more guards filling the room.]

Gem Thinks - "Where are all these bastards coming from?"

[He sees that these guys have the energy guns in hand. He also sees Willie and company leaving the scene, with Natasha and Victor.]

Gem - "Oh-no you don't!"

[He stretches to get to them but, he gets shot by one of the new weapons. He falls to the floor.]

Gem Thinks - "So that's what that does. It feels tingly, that must be the 'energy' part, I'm storing that. But those 'particles', they sting like a mother-fucker."

[More guards are coming-out with the energy weapons.]

Gem Thinks - "Well, as much fun as all this has been, it's taking way-too-fucking-long and that piece of shit is about to get away. Let's see if I can get all these guys at once."

[Gem turns both his arms into shields and cocoons himself, as the guards let loose with the energy blasts.]

Gem Thinks - "Oh, this is nice. I'm absorbing the energy and deflecting the particles. Almost there… just a little more power…"

[The guards continue to fire as they move towards him. When they get to him, they stop firing and try to check the damage. As they lean in for a closer inspection, they notice Gem is glowing. Gem lifts his head.]

Gem - "Thanks for charging-me-up, dick-heads. Now, it's lights out bitches."

[Gem let's out a blast of energy. Bodies go flying. Everyone is down. Gem looks at the aftermath.]

Gem Thinks - "Wow! That was fucking awesome. I think I even came a little. Fuck! I did. Great! Now I'm gonna have sticky-dick the rest of the day. I gotta pee and clear the pipe…Shit! Natasha!"

[Gem runs outside. He's too late. The helicopter is too far for him to reach.]

Gem - "Fuck!"

Gem's Conscience - "I told you."

Gem - "Oh, shut-up!"

[Gem sees a guard walking towards him.]

Gem Thinks - "Look at this dick-hole."

[As the guard nears, Gem sees that it's Michael, Lana's guard.]

Gem - "Mikey? Dude, what the fuck are you thinking?! Didn't you see what I just did in there?"

Michael - "I saw that you went ape-shit crazy and almost got your wife and friend killed. Why would you come in blazing? You should have done this in stealth mode."

Gem - "That's just great! I finally get my God-damn conscience in check, then you show up to lecture me. Why are you here, anyway? You trying to finish the job?"

Michael - "No, I wouldn't dream of hurting the man who saved my son's life."

Gem - "I'm confused, who's your son?"

Michael - "David."

[Gem still looks confused.]

Michael - "David! Lana's son David."

Gem - "Oooh...so this is your undercover assignment. Okay, then I have a question for you; why the fuck did you assholes let it get this far?!"

Michael - "I have to go home and check on David. Let's go. We'll talk in the car."

Gem - "I'm driving and if you don't start saying something that's gonna help right now, I'm throwing you out of the fucking car."

Michael - "Sure...that sounds reasonable."

[They get into a car and start driving to Michael's house.]

Gem - "Start talking."

Michael - "He's taking them to a food processing facility. Lana and Kutty are there too. That's where he wanted you to meet him tomorrow morning."

Gem - "Why a food processing plant? And why the fuck did he take Lana and Kutty too?"

Michael - "He took them because he knows they've been withholding information. I'm sure he's doing everything he can to retrieve it. As far as the location; I'm not sure but, it could have something to do with the irradiation chamber."

Gem - "What's he gonna do, nuke me?"

Michael - "It's a gamma irradiation chamber."

Gem - "What are you saying? You think I can't handle it?"

Michael - "I remember Lana saying that she didn't know what would happen if you were 'over-energized'. Gem, if an x-ray lights you up, this thing may blow you up."

Gem - "How are they planning to get me in there? I just dismembered most of his security detail."

Michael - "I wasn't privy to any details."

Gem - "I gotta make a stop."

Michael - "Really? Now?"

[Gem stops at a convenience store.]

Gem - "Wait here, I'll be right back."

[He comes out a couple of minutes later, with a bag in his hand. He gets back in the car and hands the bag to Michael.]

Gem - "Hold this please."

[Michael looks inside the bag to find a bottle of lube, hand sanitizer and an extra-long rubber glove.]

Michael - "What's this for? You having a party?"

Gem - "No, not this time. Those are for Willie. I told him that if he ever threatens my family again, I'll do to him what I did to the pigs in the show. Those things are just so I don't get my hands as dirty."

Michael - "Threatens them 'again'? You had a chance to take him out the first time and you warned him? Jesus, Gem; that's like challenging him! You don't warn him, you punish him."

Gem - "You know, you're the second person to tell me that today, and fuck you both! 'Cause I don't have a time-machine therefore, it's too late to change that now. Now, I have to focus on the task at hand."

[Gem practices inflating his hand a few times.]

Michael - "You know, you act like an immature, loopy idiot."

Gem - "What?"

Michael - "But, you're not."

Gem - "Go on."

Michael - "You're like an artist; a sculpture. Except, you just free-hand; shit, you don't even plan it. You just chisel away until the piece finds its own form."

Gem - "Wow! That was beautiful, man. Seriously, you are one eloquent mother-fucker. Thank you for giving me a good way to look at it."

Michael - "You're welcome."

Gem - "And here I thought that it was because I'm a passive/aggressive, charming, witty, charismatic, overly-functional Gemini."

Michael - "You forgot humble."

Gem - "It was implied."

Michael - "So, what are we going to do?"

Gem - "You're gonna go home, get your son to a safe place and call in the cavalry. Me, I'm gonna go to the food plant and get our people back."

Michael - "Any idea how?"

Gem - "Not yet. I'll just do whatever the situation requires, as I go. Oh, and I forgot to mention, I got recordings of Willie that will help with your project. They're on my phone. Why don't you email them to yourself, just in case."

[Gem hands Michael his phone. He starts looking for the files. He accidentally hits on Gem's porn folder.]

Michael - "Oh wow! Look at all this porn."

Gem - "We don't have time for that, you pervert. Go to the voice recorder file."

Michael - "Yeah, you've got twelve-hundred porn files on your phone and I'm the pervert."

Gem - "What do you want? I like variety."

[Michael finds the recordings and emails them to himself.]

Michael - "I want to go with you. I can't just sit around and wait."

Gem - "You know, there's a pretty good chance that this will all turn to shit."

Michael - "That's why I need to be there."

Gem - "No, that's why you need to not be there. How many of his parents can your son afford to lose today?"

Michael - "What about your kids? What about their parents?"

Gem - "Thanks to me and the shenanigans of Mr. dick-face Dietrich, my kids and I don't have a choice. At this point, nobody involved does. All our roles are set, we just have to play them out and hope for the best."

Michael - "Even the glove and the lube?"

Gem - "Especially the glove in the lube!"

[They pull up to Michael's house. Michael gets out of the car.]

Michael - "You sure about this?"

Gem - "Nope."

Michael - "Do you want to take a moment, to think it over."

Gem - "Nope."

Michael - "I really hope you know what you're doing."

Gem - "Don't worry, Michael."

[Gem begins to drive off.]

Gem - "So do I."

CHAPTER EIGHT:

RESTORATION

There's usually an argument going on in my head, between me and what I'm pretty sure is my conscience. Either that or some tiny dude got into my head, just to bother me and contradict everything I want to do. But not this time; this drive I made in absolute silence. We both know what needs to be done. I think part of me, really misses this side of me.

[Gem sees the food processing plant. He parks his car out of sight and proceeds to sneak into the building through the roof. He lands on a catwalk and surveys the scene.]

Gem Thinks - "Let's see what we're working with here."

[He sees two guards by the entrance. And, what looks like another lab set-up on a loft. He can't see everything going on inside but, he does see Willie and a bunch of guys in lab coats bustling around. That's where the action is, that's probably where his people are.]

Gem Thinks - "How many fucking labs does this guy have? My crew is probably in there too. I need to cause a ruckus to get whoever else is in there, to come out."

[Gem drops from the catwalk and lands right behind the guards. They quickly turn toward him. Gem shoots out his fists and knocks them both out.]

Gem Thinks - "There. Silent but, violent."

[He lifts the guards to a ledge above the lab's interior windows and slowly lowers them, by their feet. Willie and the others in the lab see the beaten bodies being lowered in front of the window and come out to see what's happening.]

Gem - "Excuse me sir, do these assholes belong to you?"

[Willie is standing there, unamused.]

Gem - "No?"

[He flings the guards / they scream as they fly through the air / Smack! against a wall / then fall to the floor with a thump.]

Gem - "Don't worry, I wouldn't have claimed them either."

[Gem jumps off the ledge, does a flip and lands in front of the lab window, just a few feet away from Willie.]

Gem Thinks - "Stuck-it!"

Willie - "This really isn't your style, Mr. Gem. You don't like to get your hands dirty."

Gem - "Oh, that all changed when you decided to go after my family. Plus, I came prepared."

[Gem plops a bottle of hand sanitizer on a table.]

Gem - "Oh, I also brought something special, just for you. Do you remember what I said I'd do to you, if you ever used my family as leverage?"

[Gem pulls out his rubber glove and puts it on past his elbow.]

Gem - "Well, I came prepared for that too. Oh, and this."

[Gem pulls out a bottle of lube and starts lubing the glove.]

Gem - "Well, this really isn't for your comfort, it's mostly for the gloves protection. We wouldn't want it tearing during the process because, it's gonna get messy. This is going to be fun. My only fear is that one of us may enjoy this too much. Though I doubt it's gonna be you. But don't worry, I'll try to hold my excitement and go slow at first. I don't want to finish before I had a chance to enjoy my moment."

Willie - "As much as I'd hate to ruin your 'moment' for you, I do believe you've forgotten about a couple of things, during all of the excitement."

[Willie motions toward the back of the lab. Gem looks over and sees Natasha, Victor, Lana and Kutty, standing there, two guards behind them with their guns drawn. Gem looks at them, then at his dripping glove; then back at them and back at the glove.]

Gem - "Here, hold this."

[Gem throws his lubed glove at Willie's face and it sticks with a "splat". He starts towards Natasha and Victor, staring at the nervous guards behind them. Then, BAM!!! A big, metal fist punches him in the chest, causing it to crater and knocking him off of the loft. As Gem's flying through the air from the hit, he sees a large, pale-gold, metal figure standing where he just was.]

Gem Thinks - "What the fuck was that? And who the fuck is that?"

[Smash! Gem hits a wall and falls to the floor.]

Gem - "Ouch."

[The figure jumps off of the loft and hero-lands in front of Gem. Gem is looking at him as he's picking himself up. The figure's metallic face peels back, it's The Specialist.]

Gem - "Oh, hey-there Sauer-boy. I was wondering where you were."

[The Specialist does not reply. He's just standing there in a fighting stance.]

Willie - "You see Mr. Gem, the last few weeks were not a complete waste of time. Sure, we had some setbacks and a few unplanned mishaps..."

Gem - "You mean like, the exploded bodies I saw in your lab?"

Willie - "Yes..."

[Willie looks at the scientists. They lower their heads in shame.]

Willie - "...like those. We've obviously gone to extreme measures in our attempts to duplicate your 'accident'. The problem was, too many variables. Your 'facility' had so much shit in it, besides the silver, that we could not find the right combination. We even got samples of the water from your basement. That too turned out useless because, it had already been 'activated' outside of a body. No matter what we tried, we could not make the silver disperse into every cell in the body. However, as you can see by Mr. Sauer, we were successful in fusing metal into the skin cells. Now, what you see here is a titanium-gold alloy, bonded to each of his skin cells. In essence, his entire body is protected by molecular scales that are nearly impossible to penetrate, especially with metal as soft as silver. See, while our competitors are making exoskeletons that one must put on, I, with your help of course, have created an exoskeleton that one can become. We've also woven in nitinol wires, to act as actuators, for added speed, endurance and strength."

Gem - "Interesting. But nitinol requires a power source."

Willie - "You're right, it does. Mr. Sauer, would you be so kind? "

[The Specialist turns his back towards Gem. The metal scales pull back, to reveal a power pack, which has been implanted below the skin.]

Willie - "Ultra-capacitor batteries. They're thin, light-weight, flexible and ironically, silver based."

Gem - "Oh, that's very nice. I'm impressed. We'll take five, please. And skip the bagging, we'll just put them on now."

Willie - "It's nice to see you keep your sense of humor about, in such a time of crisis."

Gem - "Thanks. It's a coping mechanism."

Willie - "Cope with this, Mr. Gem. Since you are unwilling to cooperate with my plan, going forward, you have moved yourself from the asset column, over to the liability column. I detest unproductive liabilities. And unfortunately, your associates have become liabilities as well. So, after I have Mr. Sauer deliver your severance package to you, I will throw in your friends, as a little bonus. He really enjoys that line of work and unlike you, he's been a model employee."

[Willie and Sauer look at each-other and smile proudly.]

Gem - "This is awkward. Do you two need a moment alone?"

Willie - "And lastly, we'll bring in your children and see if we can finish our work, with them."

[Gem stands angry and quiet.]

Willie - "What's the matter, Mr. Gem? No funny remarks? Has your coping mechanism had too much to cope with?"

Gem - "You just worry about keeping that glove lubed. I'll be needing it in a minute."

[Gem shoots his spear-tipped arm, out at The Specialist's face. The titanium-gold alloy transforms just in time. Gem's hand bends as it hits it.]

Gem Thinks - "Shit! That could be a problem."

[Gem goes into attack mode. He lunges into every potentially weak spot, at once; eyes, nose, mouth, ears, groin; all his "probes" bend and deflect.]

The Specialist - "Now, it's my turn."

[He quickly grabs Gem by the bent limbs, spins him in the air and throws him against a far wall. Gem smacks the wall, peels away and falls to the floor.]

Gem - "Ouch."

[Gem gets up and runs at The Specialist / jumps at full speed / rolls into a sphere, mid-air and knocks The Specialist into a wall, hard, leaving an indent.]

Gem - "You like that? I call it the Cannonball."

[The Specialist walks around Gem until he positions himself in line with Gem and the big metal door of the irradiation chamber. Gem looks behind him.]

Gem Thinks - "That must be the irradiation chamber. Does this guy think he's just gonna push me in there?"

[Gem looks around for a power source. Found it. The large light fixtures thirty feet above him. The Specialist runs at him / Gem leaps to the light fixture / Specialist misses / Gem shoots his hand through the light and into its socket and shoots a bolt of electricity at The Specialist. It has no effect.]

Gem Thinks - "Great! He's like a fuckin' Faraday cage. All the electricity went around the outside of his body and into the floor. Now what?"

[Gem looks down and sees The Specialist bending both ends of a metal rod into hooks. He begins to spin the rod, slowly, patiently.]

Gem - "Is that it? Show's over? I'm getting the hook?"

The Specialist - "You have no parts left to play, in this story."

That was a good one. I have to remember it, in case I get out of here alive and wanna say some mean shit to someone, before I fuck them up. Ooo, maybe to Willie.

[Gem stretch-jumps towards Willie / The Specialist jumps-up and hooks him, mid-flight. He spins him at a breakneck speed. It's too fast, the centrifugal force is too great, Gem can't get off the hook. The Specialist throws him into the chamber. Gem is disoriented, dizzy, can't even stand straight. The door is closed. Gem's trying to get to the door.]

Gem - "Come on guys, can't we talk about this?"

[He falls over. Looks at a pallet of fruit in front of him. It's labeled "Kumquats".]

Gem - "Hey, did you guys know that Kumquats are a real thing? And they look nothing like what their name would imply. I always thought it was just something you call someone when they're being a dumb-ass. Who knew?"

[Willie comes on over the intercom in the chamber.]

Willie - "Do you know what happens to a battery when it's grossly overcharged? The molecules inside become too excited, too unstable. They rearrange themselves in order to return to the lowest energy state. And that, causes structural breakdown. Good-bye, Mr. Gem. Just think of this as our last research experiment."

[Gem is getting up and looking around for a way out.]

Gem Thinks - "What a waste. There so much more I could have..."

[As Willie and Gem's crew watch on a CCTV monitor, The Specialist flips the switch. Gem sees a blinding, white light, hears a blasting, high-pitched sound in his ears, his body heats up and he begins to glow a fiery orange-red. He sees his body disassembling into pieces, he can't pull them back. Then, with a bright flash, his body separates into millions of tiny spheres. They pull away from him, floating through the air, until they drop to the floor, in unison. Still hot, still glowing. Natasha gasps, as a tear rolls down her cheek.]

So, this is it? This is death? I really thought it'd be a lot more interesting than this. Warm light and peaceful feeling, my ass. The light's blinding, I'm hot as hell and more pissed-off than ever. Wait, the light is dimming a bit. I can see but, not like usual. Everything's all pixely but, I'm beginning to make out images of my surroundings. I can hear voices through vibrations in my body, which as far as I can tell, is that stuff that looks like glowing grains of sand, scattered everywhere. Some of the fainter pieces are starting to lift from the floor and gravitate to me. Willie was right about the first part, and it sucked. But this, I don't know what this is. Maybe a chromosome connection, quantum entanglement? Whatever it is, I can feel them and I sense that they can feel me. Am I about to get another chance? Can I regroup?

[Gem's body begins to reassemble as the tiny, glowing spheres swirl around and coalesce. Each piece finding its proper place. Meanwhile, Willie is talking to someone on his phone.]

I'm feeling better already. I can see Sauer in his new digs, heading towards Natasha. I can hear Willie talking on his phone.

Willie - "...if you'd be so kind, please administer the serum to the boys. Yes, both of them. Don't worry about Mr. Gem, he's been eliminated. I should be there in time for their awakening."

Serum? What fucking serum?! Is that what woke me up too? Okay, that's it! I can't wait till I'm back together. I'm gonna molecularly-slip my way out of this place and kick some fuckin' ass!

[Gem starts to the door, not yet completely reassembled. He's still glowing, his 'pieces' still loosely held together, still gravitating back, following him as he moves. One of the guards in the lab sees that Gem's still very much alive, on the CCTV monitor. He alerts the others. The Specialist jumps off the loft, grabs his hook and stands by the chamber door. Gem walks right through the door, with some of him still following behind him. Everyone is on the loft, looking on in amazement.]

Gem - "That was sweet. I can think of a million situations where that would come in useful. I gotta see about getting one of those for the house. Victor?"

Victor - "I check into it."

Gem - "Great! Thanks."

[Gem hears a loud grunt. He looks over and sees it's The Specialist, swinging his hook at him. He swings again; the hook passes right through Gem's body. Taking a few, straggling pieces with it but, they quickly return to their proper places.]

Gem - "Uh, did you not just see me walk right through a metal door? That shit's not gonna work this time. I'm charged and that means that I can do stuff that I don't even know I can do."

[The Specialist throws his hook in frustration. He comes at Gem, full force; kicking, punching, grabbing - nothing. Gem's just standing there, letting him do his thing.]

Gem - "Really, dude? Why don't you just relax, before you hurt yourself?"

[The Specialist stops his vain assault. He's angry, frustrated, desperate to punish Gem for nullifying his victory. He looks at Gem, then at Natasha.]

Gem - "Don't even think about it, asshole!"

[The Specialist leaps at Natasha / Gem stretches his arm / hand penetrates the armor / and with a bright, fiery flash, all the organic material inside the suit, vaporizes. Tiny scales rain to the floor.]

Gem Thinks - "Shit! I think I'm outta juice."

[He looks at the pile of metallic scales on the floor.]

Gem Thinks - "It was worth it."

[Gem's no longer glowing. He jumps to the loft and lands near Willie.]

Gem - "Where's my glove, Willie? I told you I was gonna need it soon."

Willie - "Now, now, Mr. Gem. You wouldn't want to do anything rash, would you?"

[Willie motions toward Gem's wife and friends. There is still a guard behind them.]

Willie - "Let's not forget, I'm still holding some cards, too."

[Gem, while still looking at Willie, throws out a large, silver-fist punch and smashes the guard into a wall. Willie tells his last guard to go and stand behind Natasha. The guard very reluctantly, nervously and slowly walks over to Gem's wife. He holds out his gun, in his shaking hand. Gem looks at him, then back at Willie. Guard breathes a sigh of relief. BAM!!! Gem puts him through the same wall, right next to the first guy.]

Gem - "It looks like you're running out of cards to play."

Willie - "Oh, I may still have something in the hole."

Gem - "Don't worry, I already took care of your dick-heads at the hospital."

Willie - "Not all of them."

Gem Thinks - "What the fuck is he talking about? Who's left?"

Willie - "Besides, you have a more pressing issue to concern yourself with."

[Willie hold-up his phone.]

Willie - "I too, have a drastic backup plan."

Gem Thinks - "I had a drastic plan? I thought it was more like a goal."

Willie - "Every thirty minutes, I receive a text message. If I do not respond with a special code within five minutes, there will be a tragic explosion in your children's room. It's been fifteen minutes since the last correspondence, the hospital is at least fifteen minutes away. Even if you left right now, you wouldn't make it there in time."

Gem - "Call it off, Willie!"

[Gem starts at Willie.]

Michael - "Everybody Freeze!"

[Gem looks over, it's Michael with several other G-men.]

Michael - "Gem, stand-down. With what we have on this asshole, he's going to be locked away for a long time."

Gem - "Yeah, well, right now, I'm not too worried about that. What I am worried about, is that fucking douche-bag, literally holding my boys' lives in his hand."

[Gem and Willie stare at each-other.]

Gem - "Do the right thing, Willie."

Willie - "I'm afraid it's too late for that, Mr. Gem. I guess I can take solace in the notion that tomorrow, when I'm on a yacht planning my next venture, you will be planning your children's funeral."

Gem - "They had nothing to do with anything."

Willie - "Don't you see, they had everything to do with it. They, were the future."

Gem Thinks - "What the fuck does that mean?"

[Willie looks at Gem with a grin and throws his phone. Gem leaps off the loft, stretching for it, misses it. The phone hits the floor and breaks into pieces. Gem looks back at the loft. Willie is laughing as he's being escorted by a couple of agents. Gem jumps back on the loft.]

Gem Thinks - "Fuck. This. Shit!"

[Gem thrusts out his arm / it's extending toward Willie / up his ass / lifting him up from the floor / he's screaming / face turning bright red / abdomen expanding / shirt buttons popping off / BOOM!!! / Willie explodes / blood sprays everywhere / pieces of Willie fly at the on-lookers / his head smacks a wall and falls into a trash can. Everyone is flabbergasted. Gem's unused glove sitting on a ledge, dripping lube.]

Gem Thinks - "Disgusting, but necessary."

[Everyone's staring at Gem. He still has the remains of Willie's ass, pants and underwear, on his arm; just above his elbow. Gem's grossed out. He thins his arm to let the ass slide off but, it's just squeaking down, slowly.]

Gem Thinks - "Damn it! I was supposed to be getting my non-stick coating today. Everyone's watching, this is getting awkward."

[He flings his arm in frustration. The ass pops-off, flies through the air and splats on a far wall.]

Gem Thinks - "If this gets any sicker, I'm gonna hurl. I need to wipe my hand on something."

Head Agent - "You stupid fuck! What the hell was that? Arrest that idiot!"

[The agents move in on Gem.]

Gem - "Anyone who touches me, gets what he got."

[They stop and back-off. Gem steps right up to the head agent's face.]

Gem - "I just rid the world of an asshole who had no problem killing people, even innocent children, to get what he wants. If anything, I should be pissed at you for not taking care of him sooner, so we didn't have to go through this shit."

[Gem wipes his arm and hand on the head agent's suit.]

Gem - "Now, if you'll excuse me, thanks to your long list of fuck-ups, I have to go save my kids. And if you try to stop me again, I will do things to you, that will make what I did to him, look like a good alternative."

Head Agent - "Get this man to his kids."

Michael - "Gem, we have choppers, ours and Dietrich's. We can fly you to the hospital."

[They get on the choppers and head to the hospital. One of the agents recognizes Victor.]

Agent - "Victor Petrov, how did you get mixed-up in this?"

Victor - "I was kidnapped, by that piece of shit, who's piece of ass, Gem just throw on wall."

Agent - "I see."

[They get in to the helicopters. Gem checks the time; 10 minutes left.]

Michael - "We should contact the hospital to have them evacuate the area."

Gem - "No! Willie said he still had someone there. If they see the commotion, they might do something themselves. Just tell them to have the helipad ready and the door to the roof open."

[One of the agents makes the call.]

Agent - "It's all set."

[They're nearing the hospital. Three minutes left. Coming in for the landing. Gem jumps out at fifty feet, shoulder-rolls, springs through the open door and jumps down the stairs. He bursts through the door on his kids' floor, runs down the hall and into their room. Boys are still okay. Gem frantically searching for the bomb. He checks under the beds, closet, drawers, nothing. He sees a large, stuffed bear, that wasn't there yesterday. He rips it open; there's the bomb! Three seconds left, no time to think. Gem wraps himself around the bomb, BOOM! He was able to contain the blast. Gem's disoriented, vision blurred, ears ringing. Someone walks in and places a bag on the floor in the middle of the room. Gem still can't tell what's happening. He hears a voice say, "Better luck in your next lives." Then, a sudden sound, like metal going through bone. His eyes focus. He sees the man before him, it's Mendelson, the physician assistant. Gem looks down and sees several long blades, sticking out of Mendelson's chest and torso. He's holding something that looks like a detonator button. Gem looks behind him, Natasha's standing there with a shocked look on her face. He takes the detonation device out of Mendelson's hand, grabs him by the head and peels him off of the blades, letting his body fall to the floor. Natasha's staring at her hands in disbelief. The rest of the crew is standing in the doorway, they too are in shock.]

Gem - "I fucking knew it! That's my girl!"

Gem Thinks - "Is it wrong for me to be turned-on right now? See, this is why you don't wear a spandex suit."

[Natasha, still looking at her bloodied hands, retracts them and goes to wash-up. She's still in shock. Gem follows her to the sink and washes his hands too. Lana starts to check the boys' status.]

Natasha - "I don't know what happened. I just reached out to grab him and everything else just happened."

Gem - "That's because you didn't over think it. You killed him with your heart, not your brain. That's so sweet."

[Alarms start going-off on the boys' monitors. Heart rate up, pulse up, pressure up, bodies start to quiver.]

Lana - "Their bodies are going into shock. It's probably from whatever serum Wilhelm had that asshole give them. We have to defibrillate them."

[Lana grabs the defibrillator paddles.]

Gem - "No! I'll do it. How much power do I need?"

Lana - "It's hard to tell. Anywhere from 200 to 1,700 volts."

Gem - "Fuckin' really? Can you be any more vague?"

Lana - "That's just how it is. You have to start lower and step it up."

Natasha - "Gem, please, let her do it. She knows what she's doing."

Gem - "No fucking way! It's my fault they're here and I'm not gonna let anyone else carry my guilt, if things go bad. I brought them here and I'm gonna get them out."

Natasha - "Gem..."

Gem - "Please, I can do this. I can sense them. I can feel them calling out to me. Natasha, it has to be me."

[Natasha nods her head and steps aside. Gem forms each of his hands into paddles and places them on the boys' chests. He gets on his knees and shoots his foot into a socket, to charge-up.]

Lana - "Start with a small burst."

[Gem zaps the boys, nothing. He tries again with more energy, nothing.]

Lana - "More power!"

[He zaps them again. Their shaking gets violent.]

Lana - "It's now or never!"

[Gem is looking at them. Time slows down. He can feel them; their pain, their fear. He closes his eyes and sees them playing, happy, alive. The lights dim. His heart begins to glow a neon-blue. The light splits in two, travels down his arms and into the boys. The jolt knocks-out all the other equipment in the room. The boys stop shaking. Gem feels their hearts beating. He smiles and drops his head in relief. Sammy moves, then Jeffrey. Sammy opens his eyes, sees his father crying.]

Sammy - "Papa, why are you crying?"

[Jeffrey opens his eyes too, looks around the room.]

Jeffrey - "Hey, where are we?"

Gem - "We're at the hospital. There was an accident at the lab."

[The boys look at each-other.]

Sammy - "Was it our fault?"

Gem - "No, it was mine."

Jeffrey - "Did we finish our chore?"

Gem - "Yeah, it's done."

Sammy - "Then you still owe us french fries!"

[Gem starts laughing and hugging and kissing the boys, profusely. Natasha does the same, as she wipes the tears from her eyes.]

I am fucking exhausted. I think I need to sit for a bit.

[Gem sits on a chair and looks at his family. They're whole again. Natasha comes up to him.]

Natasha - "Are you okay?"

[Gem's looking at his boys. He's trying to spot silver rings in their eyes. Then, he sees it. First in Sammy and then in Jeffrey. He imagines the cool stuff they'll do together. He smiles big.]

Gem - "Yeah, I'm fucking awesome."

[Then, Gem starts thinking of what it will be like to raise these two boys, now that they have powers. He imagines parents, teachers…the police, complaining about crazy things they are doing.]

Gem Thinks - "Oh fuck."

The End...?

CHAPTER NINE:

REFLECTIONS

So, as it turns out, everyone in the house got the silver thing. Good thing we didn't have a fucking cat. Is there a moral to this story? Not really. If I had to do it all again, knowing what I know now, I'd probably do it all the same. All's well, when it ends well. Why change it? And as for me, it hasn't done shit to change me. In fact, besides the silver thing, I'm more the same than ever, maybe just a little more dangerous. But I will say this: Life is short. You never know when the rug will get pulled-out from under you. You have to appreciate it, make the most of every moment and most importantly, enjoy the ride. 'Cause otherwise, what's the fucking point?

Oh, and as for what I wanted from Lana after the surgery…I guess you'll just have to wait for the next book to find out.